Runaway Heart

Hearts of Three Rivers
#1

AMITY LASSITER

For Angel.

Hearts of Three Rivers

Runaway Heart

Homecoming Heart

ACKNOWLEDGMENTS

I need to thank my mom and daddy. If I am honest, I've had more than my fair share of silly ideas in this lifetime, and they've always been sure that, once they confirmed I *actually* meant it, they supported me 100%, even if failure was imminent.

Mr. Lassiter believed I was a writer even when *I* didn't believe I was a writer. For his ability to wait for me when I'm on a roll, understand that I didn't change out of my pyjamas all day because I had hit a sweet spot, and his tolerance for 90% of his dinners being done in the slow cooker so that I could spend less time cooking and more time writing, he deserves an award.

My sister, Shay, who in the early days understood that 'let's go for a drive.' actually meant 'let me hold you as a captive audience and figure out what the hell is wrong with my story arc', and still got into the car without the need for force.

And last but not least, the Divas of RD. Keriann, Zoe, Elle, Kate, Elianne, Mel, Jules, and too many others to name, for knowing what I needed most—whether that was a hug or a kick in the ass.

ONE

DANE BAYLOR FELT the thud of dead weight hitting the ground in the soles of his boots before he ever heard the scream.

The bay colt he had been working with skittered sideways several feet in the corral and Dane let an oath out under his breath, angry that the progress he had been making with the horse had just been undone.

"*Goddamnit*, Gage." He swore as he swung around to find the source of the noise. "What have I *told* you about scaring—"

His words cut off when he saw his five year old nephew crumpled on the ground near the six foot tall corral fence the boy had just been sitting on. He was holding one arm at an awkward angle and squealing like a kicked dog.

Dane's heart ricocheted off his ribcage as he broke out in a run to the boy. He could see Finn coming out of the heifer barn to see what all the ruckus was about. Dane reached the boy first and propped him up against a post, doing his best to quiet his squalling nephew.

"It's a long way from your heart, Gage, best quit your bellyaching now or you'll run out of breath." His words were gruff with fear, and he winced when he noticed the splinter of bone protruding through the skin. "*Goddamnit!*" He hissed under his breath.

Finn finally reached the pair, kneeling beside his brother and his nephew. He put a reassuring hand on Gage's shoulder. Narrowing his eyes at his brother, he frowned.

"Why weren't you watching him?"

"I *was* watching him. He was sitting right here." Dane was mad enough to spit nails—at his brother *and* his nephew. It had been a perfect day to get the string of colts from Reicher started and now he had to take a trip to the hospital; and not just that, but he was also being accused of negligence. "Christ. I *was* watching him, but what am I supposed to do, hover over him all day? I have as much work to do as you!"

Dane could tell his younger brother wanted to retaliate, but he clenched his jaw shut, looking pointedly at their nephew sitting between them, then back to Dane. It made Dane's blood boil. Finn could say whatever he wanted about how Dane parented Gage, but at the end of the day, between the three of them, Dane was the only one fit for the job. Noah barely had his life under control again and Finn had good days and bad since Sunny died. It was on his good days that he tended to give Dane the hardest time.

Both men looked in bewilderment at the boy,

who was still howling with pain. The neighbors would come running soon if they didn't quiet him or move him. For a fleeting moment, Dane thought about taking up his mother's offer to keep Gage so he could work on the ranch in peace. She'd raised four boys; just one would be a walk in the park, despite how difficult it seemed to be for Dane himself. As it stood now, he felt like he was shooting blind half the time. It would be a hell of a lot easier than *this*, whatever this clumsy attempt at parenting was, but he had a promise to keep.

With a heavy sigh, Dane helped Gage to his feet and the three Baylor boys hobbled toward the car.

~

"I'm just saying, Dane, you could use some help." Ella Baylor shrugged as she made a fourth pass across the hospital's waiting room floor. "I know I raised you right, but you don't have to be so damn independent."

Dane was sitting doubled over with his elbows propped on his knees in an uncomfortable hospital chair. His hat was on the chair beside him and he was still wearing the same dusty boots and faded jeans from the ranch, feeling entirely out of place in the sterile environment.

They were waiting for Gage to come out of surgery and his nerves were just about shot. Not even his mother's presence was helping. He bounced one leg anxiously. Every single thing about this situation put him on edge.

"I can do it, mama. I promised Gavin."

Ella gave him a pointed look. Even two years later, just the mere mention of his youngest brother's name shot Dane through the heart, it had to be the same for her. Maybe worse.

"Gavin never intended for you to do this all on your own, Dane. We're a family. There's no harm in me or your father coming over for a few hours a day to keep an eye on Gage while you get some work done. That's not admitting defeat. That's being smart."

"You and dad left the ranch to me so you could open the store. You did your time. I'm not going to let you be tied down to it again, whether it's to look after cattle or children."

Dane was fiercely proud of the ranch he inherited when his father had started to have heart problems. He'd grown up working alongside Caine Baylor and it was natural for him to take the reins when his parents retired into town. Finn had stayed behind to help with the work, and Noah, their younger brother, had gone with Caine and Ella to apply his business smarts to their operation. Even so, any one of them would have dropped everything to come to his aid if he only asked; he just didn't think they should have to.

"You don't understand, Dane. I would *love* to do it. Your father would love it, too. Stop being so stubborn." Ella crossed her arms and Dane nearly laughed aloud.

Everything he had learned about being

stubborn, he had learned from his mother. She just called it 'independent'. The running joke in town was that nobody had been able to control Ella growing up and Caine was the only man who wouldn't bother to try, so that was why they had married. Once she got an idea into her head, you either went with it or got bowled over.

Dane looked up at his mother. Age wore well on her. Her once-blond hair had begun to thread with silver long ago and she wore it proudly instead of trying to hide it. Her body was wiry and strong, a testament to years as a rancher's wife, throwing calves and bales of hay alongside the man she loved. He was told he had inherited her eyes—the same color as thunderclouds reflecting on a still lake. She looked well, but she and his father had earned their retirement through every drop of sweat and sleepless minute tending stock they'd put in.

"If you really think I should have someone keeping Gage, I'll hire someone. You can visit as often as you like, but I won't saddle you with that burden."

"Dane. It's not a bur—"

Dane stood abruptly, quieting her. His mind was made up. Why the thought hadn't occurred to him sooner he didn't know, but now it seemed like the best idea he'd had in a long time.

"You can come over as often as you want, but the hired homemaker will be his official caretaker— that way if you need to go to town or you feel sick, you have no obligation to come over. You raised four boys, mama, and you did a fine job, but you've earned your rest."

Ella conceded with a tired nod of her head. It was probably the only battle with her Dane would win in his entire life, but he'd take the victory.

TWO

Homemaker wanted, room & board provided.
Must be good with children.
Call 555-8705

THE AD ON the wall of the Laundromat was short and sweet. Ever optimistic, Ren Maddock convinced herself that meant the job would be simple. She snatched the paper off the wall without a second thought and stuffed it into her pocket.

"What's that?" Kerri was momentarily disturbed from the music blaring over her headphones when she saw her sister's quick movement.

"A job," Ren replied, but Kerri had already gone back to her music.

She had assured Kerri, when they moved, that there was no worry about money. In fact, that had been one of her bargaining points to talk her sister into being uprooted from yet another school, home, and set of friends. They could live like queens in the sleepy town of Three Rivers. It was all farmers and ranchers, housing would be cheap and plentiful, everything inexpensive and easy.

Kerri still put up an indignant fight but Ren had the final say, as always. She would have loved to be able to set down permanent roots somewhere so her sister could finally adjust and become a useful member of society but she hadn't exactly had a choice this time around. She was hopeful Three Rivers could be a permanent home for them. It was just a matter of what would be more harmful in the long run—letting their past catch up with them or uprooting her continually.

Shaking her thoughts from heading down a decidedly destructive path, Ren opened the triple load dryer that held the majority of the sisters' worldly possessions within and tested the dryness of the clothes. Satisfied, she pulled them out onto a nearby table and began folding methodically.

Of all the different cities they had lived in, one running theme comforted Ren. Laundromats were the same. The harsh lighting, the Formica-topped tables, the smell of detergent and fabric softener. The same tired people who dragged bags and baskets full of their dirty laundry out in public when they had a rare spare moment. It was a certain breed of people that used Laundromats and Ren had it down to such a fine science she could have probably recognized them on the street.

Kerri bobbed her head to music they could both hear reverberating from her mp3 player and began to fold the 'easy' clothes. Towels. Pants. The story of their lives. Ren looked after the messy stuff; folding shirts and underwear, and matching socks together. Kerri glided through, oblivious to the challenges her older sister faced. Ren worked damn hard to keep as much of it off of her sister's shoulders as she could.

"Are we going to look at apartments this afternoon?" Kerri pulled her headphones off and the music became louder, filling the air between them.

Ren looked up, but her hands kept folding. It was comforting, like a second nature to her.

"I want to see about this homemaker job first. It's got room and board provided, so we just might get lucky."

Kerri rolled her eyes.

"I *don't* want to live with some old lady in a wheelchair, getting that sick baby powder smell all over me and eating prunes for breakfast, Rennie. And I *know* you don't want to change diapers for a living. Come on. Let's just get an apartment and find you another job."

Ren almost smiled at her sister's protests and reached out to poke her on the arm playfully.

"A job is a job, Ker. We're not in a position to be picky, and if we can kill two birds with this one stone, I guess you'll just have to go to Three Rivers High smelling like an old lady. Why don't you finish up here and I'll go call."

Leaving her sister to facecloths and hand towels, Ren headed for a quiet alcove away from the noise of the washers and dryers and pulled out her cell phone. It was old and she had to twist her mouth just the right way to make it work, but it still made calls and texts just fine and that was the important part. She keyed the number in and a kind feminine voice answered on the second ring.

"Baylor residence."

Ren took a deep breath. She hated talking on the phone, but she put her best voice forward, getting straight to business.

"Hi, my name is Ren Maddock. I'm calling about the homemaking position I saw listed on the bulletin board at the laundromat. I'd love to come by for a chat if the position is still available."

"You're the first call, but why don't you stop by around two?"

Ren scribbled directions to the home and a fax number for her resume on the back of the ad, and thanked the woman for her time without asking any further details. A job was, after all, a job.

THREE

"HOLY *SHIT*!" KERRI exclaimed as Ren turned her ancient GMC Jimmy into the driveway of the address she'd been given earlier. Dirt road would have been a more accurate description, as there was no house in sight, just rolling fields of uncut timothy hay. As they made their way down the bumpy path, a large house came into view, along with two barns, several outbuildings, and rail fences.

The house was impressive; a two story mix of wood and shingle with a stone chimney running up one end. A covered porch stretched the length of the house. A new-looking pickup truck was parked in front, along with an equally pristine-looking car in an identical silver hue. Ren felt acutely self-conscious about her old Jimmy. It had seen better days and she'd said an extra-long prayer to get it across country to Three Rivers, but it had been as vital a presence in her life for the last four years as

Kerri had been.

"Well, at least there's a lot of space," Kerri said, rolling down her window to stick her head out and get a better look. An old looking, long haired dog with no tail and floppy ears approached, wiggling his hindquarters with joy at the arrival of the newcomers. Ren slammed on the brakes to avoid hitting him but he had already sashayed out of the way, obviously knowledgeable about vehicles.

"You can say that again." Ren shifted the vehicle into park, took a calming breath, and slipped her sunglasses off. She smoothed her hands over her unruly auburn hair and straightened her modest top, opening the door. "You stay here. I won't be too long, I hope."

Kerri's only response was to turn up the music she'd been playing the entire ride loud enough that the dog cocked his head with curiosity at the tinny sound emitting from the car. He quickly lost interest in the human remaining inside of the car and made his way to Ren, performing the exact same wiggle routine around her feet as he had around the car. She moved carefully to avoid tripping and eventually gave up and stooped to scratch behind the dog's ears. He closed his eyes in pleasure.

She startled a bit when she heard the door to the big house swing open.

"Rex! Come on, leave her alone." The man who just about filled up the door frame patted his thigh and the dog made a grumbling noise, giving her a regretful look before slinking off.

Straightening, she sucked in a tight breath as her eyes slid over his body.

He was well over six feet tall with close cropped blond hair. Broad shoulders tapered down into a narrow waist that wore a pair of faded Wranglers slung low. A black t-shirt clung tight to his torso, exemplifying every ridge of muscle on his body. He had a pair of dusty cowboy boots with spurs on his feet. His exposed arms were tanned and well-muscled, his hands had obviously seen a significant day or two of work, and his eyes reminded her of a storm coming on. Ren would have bet five dollars his name would have shown up next to 'cowboy' in the dictionary. Her mouth went a little bit dry. *Yum.*

"You must be Ren." He extended his hand before she even made it to the steps of the porch.

"I am." He was most definitely not the person who had answered the phone earlier that morning. Ren finally reached him and took his hand. His grip was firm, confident. He was a man who exuded power in a quiet, unelaborate way.

"Dane Baylor. Come on in."

Ren followed him into the house, appreciatively watching the muscles in his back move under his dark shirt. She couldn't imagine that he needed any care—but she sure wouldn't have minded if he was her charge. *First order on the list... sponge bath.*

It had been some time since Ren had enjoyed any carnal pleasures. Her first concern for the last four years had been Kerri. Romance, or more specifically in this case, lust, played second fiddle, if it got an opportunity to make a noise at all. Lust would, once again, be shoved into a closet for the sake of other, more important responsibilities, like acquiring and keeping a job.

"So Mr. Baylor, could you tell me a little bit about the position?" Ren settled herself in an offered chair at the butcher block table that dominated most of the open kitchen. It was an older style room, with dark oak cupboards, but surprisingly modern appliances. She wasn't a very sophisticated cook, but she knew her way around the kitchen and could see herself comfortable in this one.

"Please, call me Dane. Coffee?" He offered the pot from the coffeemaker and a blue clay mug. She nodded and he poured, tipping his head toward the sugar and cream on the table. Helping herself, she spooned two sugars into her coffee and ignored the cream.

"Dane, then." Ren smiled at how easily it rolled off her tongue as she stirred her coffee. "What kind of homemaking exactly are you looking for?"

He sat opposite her at the table with a mug of his own coffee, opting to drink it black.

"My nephew, Gage, lives here with me. Obviously, it's a big house with lots of places for a boy to get into trouble. I really just need someone to make sure he's fed, clothed, and not running wild while I tend to the ranch." He offered her a bone melting smile, his eyes crinkling with crows' feet at the edges and a dimple appearing on his left cheek. "The compensation is more than fair, and a room in the house is included."

Ren nodded. It sounded fair enough—simple, like the ad had led her to believe. She prepared herself for the next difficult point of conversation.

"About the accommodations... I do have a special requirement, if I were to get the job."

He tipped his head wordlessly, waiting, and she continued, attempting to choose her words carefully.

"I'm the primary caretaker for my fifteen year old sister. As I wouldn't have accommodations outside of this house, I would need to bring her with me. She's no trouble, honestly. We could share a room. And you could deduct from my salary for extra groceries." Ren held her breath and waited for the other shoe to drop. Understandably, this was the type of job for someone with no other commitments, least of all one that would require additional resources from her employer.

Dane raised a brow and rose from the table, bringing his coffee mug with him.

"Let me show you the house, Ren."

She got to her feet and followed him, perplexed that he'd ignored her revelation as he headed through a long hall and up a stairway.

"The master bedroom is downstairs—and so is Gage's bedroom—makes it easier for me to keep an eye on him and on the stock at the same time. Up here..." He gestured as they arrived at the top floor. "Is pretty much unused. There are four bedrooms. You can take your pick and your sister..."

"Kerri." She supplied after a moment.

"...Kerri. She can also choose her own space. It will work out just fine. The school bus comes by the end of our road every day. Gage will be starting school in September."

At his invitation, Ren poked her head inside one of the bedrooms, which was fully furnished in tasteful rustic decor. Far more lavish than anything she could ever imagine decorating on her own, the room intimidated her. Ren looked up at the man who stood in the door frame with her, close enough to smell his masculine, woodsy aftershave.

"Perhaps we should carry on with the interview...." Ren couldn't let herself hope that it would be this simple, but she found herself imagining her personal items in the room.

"Interview's over, Ren. Pending a quick background check, you're hired." He held out his hand to seal the deal and she reluctantly put hers into it, acutely aware of the calloused fingertips brushing against the pulse in her wrist. He had to have been able to feel it speeding a mile a minute. She frowned, trying to discern exactly what kind of thought process was going on behind those eyes, but she couldn't figure out a damn thing.

"We run two hundred head of Limousin cattle, so I'm usually busy working stock. Between the cows and the quarter horses we breed and train, I've got my brain in eight thousand places all at once, especially when we get to calving and foaling season. It's going to be a goddamn relief, excuse my language, to have even one of those eight thousand places covered. When can you move in?"

Ren didn't have the heart to tell him everything they owned was already packed in the back of Jimmy.

"When would you *like* me to move in?" He continued to stand in the doorway of the bedroom with her. What would be uncomfortably close to some obviously had no significance to him. She was the first to break, taking a step away to a more reasonable distance. Too much longer and her heart might have pounded straight out of her chest.

"The sooner the better. We're due to start calving soon and this place just about goes crazy."

"Tomorrow?" Ren held her breath—she seemed to be doing that a lot lately. She had already booked the bed and breakfast for another night, and she didn't want to seem too eager.

"Tomorrow's just fine." Dane led the way down the stairs back into the kitchen where he took Ren's empty coffee mug. "I'll give you a call if anything comes up on the background check, but otherwise, show up and we'll move you in."

"Thank you, Dane." She caught his eyes for just a moment, hoping she could convey her sincerity. Being hired for this job took care of a few of the crucial points she would have had to look after in the next couple of days in one fell swoop and it set her mind at ease. "Really."

The smile he returned made her stomach flip-flop. "You're welcome, Ren."

~

Dane poured his leftover coffee into the sink and watched Ren head back out to her car. He shook his head, clucked his tongue and sighed, an amused smile toying across his lips. Ren Maddock was something else, he just couldn't quite figure what that something else was.

Though her resume showed she'd be better suited as a waitress than a caretaker for Gage, and his mama and brothers would all give him guff for hiring a pretty face, it had only taken him about two minutes of conversation to decide to hire her. It had taken him about two *seconds* to decide he wanted to bed her. It could be difficult to abstain from mixing business with pleasure, but Dane's reckless and wanton days were over with the duties of guardianship for his nephew. He could restrain himself. He would, because this would be a good choice for Gage and he was his top priority these days.

Ren didn't get right into her car but walked past it, toward the orchard. Dane recognized a flash of red ball cap. Gage. The boy was supposed to be with Finn in the barns but the new arrivals had drawn his attention. Dane set his mug in the sink and followed her out into the yard.

Rex was yipping and wiggling around a lanky teen aged girl with the same auburn hair as Ren's. She was seated at the base of one of the bigger trees and was holding a stick she threw for the dog. He retrieved it quickly, then returned to lie by her outstretched legs, his long tongue hanging out of his mouth as he panted, giving the appearance of a satisfied grin. Old Rex had been with Dane for almost a decade now, and it only took a couple of throws before he tired out but there had once been a time when the dog was tireless and trotted along every trail and fence line Dane rode. These days, Rex had been making his best canine attempt to nanny Gage where Finn and Dane failed. Too bad none of them had been able to prevent the broken arm.

Nestled beside the teen was his nephew, a small boy with strawberry blond hair and a mess of freckles on his nose; the image of his own father when he'd been that age. He was chattering away as the girl who Dane could only assume was Kerri nodded, responding now and then with reserved one word comments.

"So how bad is the old coot?" She spoke to Ren, only noticing after she'd opened her mouth that Dane was not far behind her sister. Kerri stopped, her cheeks flushing red as she took him in.

"Not too old and not too coot-y, from what I can tell. He's only five. He might think you have cooties, though." Dane spoke up, his tone not unkind as he nodded toward his nephew. "Ren, this is Gage—Gage, this is the lady we talked about who would come to live with us and play with you while I'm busy."

The boy jumped to his feet, surprisingly agile considering the cast, and wrapped his arms around Ren's knees. Dane's chest was tight with pride.

There were moments, small as they were, that made him think he might not be entirely off the mark with his parenting strategies and this was one of them. Despite the loss in his life, Gage was still a remarkably open and loving child.

He watched as Ren crouched to Gage's level and opened her arms to give him a proper hug.

"It's nice to meet you, Gage. I'm excited to be here to play with you."

Dane's gaze swung now to the still-flustered teen at the base of the tree.

"And you must be Kerri. I'm Dane, and that," he gestured to the dog lazing happily in the grass beside her, "is Rex. And he is very happy to have you here. So am I."

Dane was sincere. The big house felt empty since his parents had moved into town and he was looking forward to a feminine presence in the home again, especially one as enticing as Ren.

FOUR

"REX! REX! THEY'RE here!" Gage nearly tripped over his feet and the dog's as he bounded down the stairs from the upper balcony where he'd been keeping watch for the Maddocks all morning.

Dane looked up from where he had been seated at the kitchen table with his mother, going over the details of the informal offer of employment he had scrawled out for Ren to sign. He'd called in a favor with the Sheriff, an old family friend, and expedited the process to do a background check. As he'd suspected, she came back clean as a whistle.

He felt like he was in junior high again, the way his heart quickened when he heard the roar of the Jimmy's well used motor in the yard.

He couldn't explain to himself and hadn't bothered to try explaining to his mother why he had hired the young woman on the spot. Something about her had spoken to him, almost before he'd even shaken her hand. Her firm grip and consistent eye contact had confirmed: this was no weak woman. Her strength and resolve made her that much more beautiful, not that she needed it.

Though she tried to hide it with her uncomplicated wardrobe of jeans, a modest V-neck top and sneakers, her body was feminine and appealing. She was not petite by any stretch of the imagination but she had an hourglass figure and a body that obviously was no stranger to hard work. Her curves were sumptuous, enough for a man to truly put his hands on. She stood only a couple of inches shorter than he did and wore her wavy auburn hair long and loose around her shoulders. It was as though she could control every part of her life, but had let her hair run wild because she needed a little excitement.

Since she was fearlessly handling a teenager, he suspected she wasn't the type of woman who would call him screaming to come and kill a spider, catch a mouse, or clean up a puddle of vomit. She might even be useful on the ranch as a hand if she weren't going to be so important in the house. He had a feeling there was much more to the story of her fifteen year old sister living with her than she had let on, or might ever tell. One way or the other, she was the type of woman he wanted—as an employee and in his bed—strong, sure, a challenge.

Ella rose as Dane did and the two of them went out onto the porch to meet the car, Gage well ahead of them, his cowboy boots pulled onto the wrong feet. Rex was a wiggling, barking, excited mess around his feet. The two of them spilled off the deck and into the driveway, tripping over one another as they went, each one making as much noise as the other.

"Watch it or you'll end up breaking the other arm!" Dane called after his nephew.

Dane drew in a breath as he watched Ren get out of the car. Damn, if she didn't look as good as she had the day before in a pair of dark washed jeans and a white t-shirt that showed just enough cleavage to be mouth-watering. *Get a grip, Baylor.*

He was no eunuch, that was for certain, but it would suffice to say Dane had other things on his mind over the last two years with Gage under his care. Ranching was a job that never got any easier, and raising a child on top of it, all alone, was a serious complication. He barely had time to shit, shower, and shave, never mind bed a woman lately.

Ella stepped off the porch ahead of him, but Gage had already made it to Ren and Kerri, meeting them in front of the car. The boy wound his good arm around Kerri's knees, closing his eyes with a satisfied smile that nearly swallowed up his whole face. Kerri's bewildered gaze passed from Dane to Ella, and finally to Ren.

"I have a yicky-yuck stuck to me." Her voice held no disdain but neither did it hold any excitement or affection. Ren laughed out loud and reached down to ruffle Gage's hair affectionately.

"Hey, what about *my* hug today?" Ren teased and Gage immediately unvelcro'd himself from Kerri and onto her older sister. The boy didn't waste any time getting familiar, that was for sure.

After giving Ren a quick squeeze, Gage stepped back with a perplexed look on his face.

"Wait, a yicky-*what*?" Before anyone could respond, he dismissed it with a shrug and grabbed Kerri's hand with his grubby one. "Uncle Dane says you can pick your own bedroom. Let me show you!"

Before Kerri could protest, Gage was pulling her toward the porch, up the steps, into the house, and out of sight. Ren watched them go with a chuckle, looking a little anxious. It was then that Ella approached, with her typical ease. The woman made anyone feel like family in ten seconds, flat.

"Ren. I'm Ella, we spoke on the phone yesterday." Forgoing a handshake, the older woman enveloped the younger in a hug. Dane saw Ren stiffen for a moment before letting herself get caught up in the warmth, compassion, and love that was his mother. "I'm sorry my husband Caine couldn't be here, but he wanted me to tell you how glad we are to have you."

~

For a moment, Ren was surprised by Ella Baylor's hug, but melted into it easily. Though she didn't know much about a mother's love based on her own experiences, Ella's entire aura was warm, comforting, and infectious.

"Well, we're glad to be here." Ren offered Ella a smile and then met Dane's gaze briefly. His slate eyes sparked slow, fixed on her—like the wind on a lake right before a storm. Every degree of her body heat pooled at the base of her belly and she looked away anxiously, turning her attention back to Ella. "We're really looking forward to learning about life on a ranch. We grew up in a pretty urban area and Kerri has never even touched a horse before."

"There's nothing better than raising a young person in the country. They grow up hard-working, responsible, and respectful, as I'm sure my boys will prove to you." She cast a teasingly warning look in Dane's direction.

"I'm sorry to run off on you—but I've got to help out with the lunch rush at the store. I just wanted to be here to welcome you into the family." She gave Dane a kiss on the cheek and squeezed Ren's shoulder lightly. "Please call me if you need *anything*—help, advice, company, coffee. Anything."

"It was nice to meet you." Ren smiled as Ella waved and got into the sedan in the yard, pulling carefully out of the drive.

Ren watched as Ella's sedan drove out of sight and then turned to find herself alone with Dane, awkwardly staring at one another across an expanse of space that seemed too far and too close all at once. What was it about this man and standing too close and looking a little too long? The way he looked at her now made her feel as though she was going to be swallowed whole if she didn't make a quick move—at the same time, she wasn't one hundred percent sure she *didn't* want to be swallowed whole by this real live cowboy.

She wanted to say something to break the

silence but couldn't think of a single thing, and tucked her hands in her pockets, almost shy. He took her cue, breaking the intense gaze.

"Let's go get the kids and I'll give you the grand tour of the ranch."

FIVE

DANE FOLLOWED REN up the stairs and toward Gage's excited chattering. Kerri's answers to his questions were sparsely worded and quiet, but the novelty of his fascination with her didn't seem to have worn off just yet. It didn't matter to Gage, who continued to carry on the mostly one sided conversation, barely pausing for a breath. Dane knew he was just happy to have someone closer to his age than his uncle who might listen to what he had to say.

The two of them were seated side by side on the bed, with Rex watching them expectantly, adding his own voice to their conversation here and there. Ren stopped abruptly in the doorway to take in the scene with a smile and Dane nearly ran straight into her. He pulled to a stop before he hit her but he was close, close enough to take in the clean, fresh, feminine smell of her with earnest hunger.

Damn. He was already knee deep in a pile of trouble. She'd only been in his home a total of about an hour and he wanted to drag her to his bedroom and ravish her without excuse or apology. He would take his time with her, tasting every inch of her satiny flesh... *Jesus.*

Apparently the side effect of having no time for women was that he turned into a rabid pervert when he finally got one up close and personal.

She looked over her shoulder at him and offered a smile that made his knees weak. He checked himself.

"Which room should I take?"

"I know just the one." Dane turned and led the way, pushing open a door at the opposite end of the hall from the feminine room Kerri had selected with Gage's help. The guest room he showed her was spacious with a queen bed, an en suite bathroom, and a second door to a back stairwell. He had actually grown up in this room, but he'd done renovations after his folks moved out and it didn't hold much semblance, decor-wise, to the room he'd once occupied. Long gone were the posters of scantily clad girls and his rodeo heroes.

"This is the largest bed in the guest rooms— it's got the bathroom and then this stairway leads to the back landing by Gage's bedroom." He paused— the landing and stairwell separated Gage's bedroom and his own. "You know, in case he has a nightmare or something."

"Does he have nightmares often?" she asked.

The question made Dane uncomfortable. He

had long felt that if anybody who knew much of anything about parenting really questioned him, he'd be found wanting. His fear of somehow tanking the ranch financially sat only marginally higher than failing Gavin on his list of things that scared the shit out of him.

It wasn't that he didn't try; it was just that he sometimes felt like there was some certain science to raising a child that he hadn't quite mastered. He filled in the gaps with unconditional love for Gage, but there was no way he would ever replace Gavin as the boy's father. Though Dane was a patient man, he could get a little gruff when he was afraid— he'd apologized a million times over for yelling at Gage when he'd fallen off the corral fence.

Gavin had been a natural father, endlessly patient with Gage. The second Gage was born, it was clear Gavin's primary purpose in life was to be that kid's dad. There had never been a second of doubt that he would raise his son to be a fine young man with manners, humor and generosity. Dane just hoped he could at least maintain that and do his brother proud.

"Not many." He shifted, desperate to change the subject, lest she find out he was a fake and a failure. "Let's get your things."

~

Ren had hoped she would be able to unload the Jimmy on her own, without Dane seeing the meager offerings that made up the entirety of their worldly possessions. The four of them went downstairs and began unloading the few bags they had between them. She pulled a battered steamer trunk out of the back with the intent to carry it in herself. The cargo was too precious to entrust to anyone else, but when Dane saw her tugging at it, he stepped in.

"Let me take that." He appeared beside her, taking one of the handles. She hesitated but then ceded to let him carry it, sliding a couple of duffel bags over her shoulders instead. Kerri carried her own backpack and duffle and Gage followed behind, insistent on carrying something. The teen had graciously bestowed her purse upon him with the hopes he would be satisfied by helping that much.

They emerged for the second load of bags to find a man in the yard throwing a stick for Rex.

He was dressed for ranch work and as tall as Dane, with the same sort of charming good looks. He had an open, welcoming expression and a smile that said he was in on the big joke that was life. His curly, dark hair was plastered to his forehead from the heat and his strong jaw was covered with what looked like a persistent five o'clock shadow, even though it was early morning. The man wiped his hands on his jeans and offered her one to shake.

"You must be the new hand... I'm sorry, my brother didn't mention your name..."

"Ren Maddock. The girl you just saw go in the house with Gage is my younger sister, Kerri. Good to meet you..."

"I'm Noah, Dane's little brother. He's got me on every other detail while he looks after you." His words were loud enough for Dane to catch and he whipped around to give his brother a playful shove in the shoulder.

"I can settle myself in if you have other things..." Ren felt acutely aware of what a big deal it was for Dane to be putting his work off to attend to her. She shifted uncomfortably—from the weight of the bag or the worry that she was being an inconvenience, she wasn't sure. Dane cut her words off easily.

"You're my first priority today. I want you to feel comfortable here and I intend to be the one to make you feel that way. And besides, this is what I pay *him* for."

The truth was, Ren wasn't sure she *could* feel comfortable here on the Baylor ranch with Dane around all the time, hovering near enough that she could smell the scent of clean linen and old leather on him, his dark eyes searing her to her core every time she turned around. She was determined to make this work though, for the sake of her sister and everything else.

She offered a smile to the younger brother. "Well, Noah, hopefully I'll see more of you around, if he doesn't keep you too busy filling in for him."

"Oh I'll keep him busy." Dane quipped, and gave his brother another playful shove as Noah winked and waved before heading off in the direction of the barns. The joviality between the two men made Ren smile. The sense of family around the Baylor ranch was clear and refreshing.

So far, the Baylors were happy to have her, and had made it a point to make her feel welcome. She hadn't had any real sense of family apart from Kerri for quite a while and although it had been disarming at first, she could get used to this feeling of being wanted, appreciated, and welcomed. Now, if she could just keep herself out of trouble, which meant staying out of Dane's way.

SIX

IT DIDN'T TAKE long for Ren to unpack her things; there wasn't much to put away. In addition to the fact that she'd never had a chance to go to college and only qualified for minimum wage jobs, the fewer things she had to throw into a bag when her mother found them and they had to uproot, the better. The most cumbersome thing they'd kept around was the small metal steamer trunk she'd filched out of her mother's home the last time she'd left.

Inside, the trunk held what little was physically left of Declan Maddock, the man who had been Ren's unfaltering superhero. As she'd prepared to leave Anita Maddock's home, Ren had collected the contents of the trunk bit by bit—a tobacco pipe, a small record player with an oak box, a worn flannel shirt that still smelled of his cologne. The most valuable item in the whole box was the Simon and Garfunkel record she had listened to countless times on her father's knee. She had learned every word to *Bridge Over Troubled Water* by the time she was five. Her fondest and most vivid memories were of him putting her to bed when she was around eight, tucking her in and singing the verses over and over until she fell asleep. It had been a comfort to her when her mother had become unkind.

Ren set the record player on one end of the long, wide dresser that took up most of one wall and plugged it in. She was just pulling out the worn record when a knock startled her and she turned to see Kerri standing in the doorway.

"Can I see?"

"Come on in." Ren moved to her bag on the bed and began to pull clothes out and look for places to put them in the walk-in closet. She was only sorry she didn't have more to put in there. Her t-shirts seemed strange hanging in a space that was obviously meant for much more, and her jeans folded over the hangers looked sad. She made a mental note to take some money out of her first pay to buy a nice dress, just so she could say she had one, and she could make the closet feel useful.

Ren noticed that Kerri, for once, didn't have her headphones hanging around her neck. She cast an upward eyebrow at her younger sister's bare neck and Kerri shrugged with a slightly guilty look.

"Gage is in my room listening to it."

Ah ha, thought Ren—already a big improvement. The younger Maddock girl had been having trouble with relationships recently, and understandably so—it seemed like the minute she laid down any positive ties in a town, they would be forced to pack everything up and move again.

"So what do you think?" Ren asked. The room was decorated in a rather unisex fashion but it was well appointed. The walls were a neutral beige and showcased a couple of pieces of framed artwork. The huge four poster bed she sat on had beautiful oak woodwork and a dark finish. A soft tan carpet enveloped her bare feet.

"My room is nice, but this room..." Kerri took the room in, then cocked a brow at her older sister with a good-natured grin. "He must save this room for when the queen visits!"

Ren rolled her eyes and nodded toward the door that led to the staircase.

"And those stairs lead down to Gage's room."

"No way!" Kerri started across the floor, pulling the door open. The staircase was well lit and covered in carpet. "I'm going down!"

Ren followed her sister down the stairs. Dane was at the bottom of them and let out a rumbling laugh as Kerri almost barreled into his broad chest.

"Figuring out the lay of the land?"

Kerri nodded, looking over her shoulder at Ren. Obviously she was not at the same kind of odds with herself when she was in Dane's presence as her older sister, but he definitely flustered the young girl. Kerri was becoming aware of the male physique, and not just the young, mostly shapeless boy band version of it. Coming to her sister's rescue, Ren eased down the stairs into the small space of the landing with the pair of them.

"Ren said this staircase came down to Gage's room." Kerri finally spoke.

Dane gestured over her shoulder at the room to the left of the staircase. Large, colorful wooden letters were arranged on the outside of the door that said 'Gage'. The door was cracked slightly open and Ren could see a mess of toys and games on the floor. She made a mental note to help him organize and keep it clean since it seemed obvious by the rest of the house that Dane was not one for clutter or disorganization. Kerri poked her head in the room and nodded approvingly.

"And this one is mine." The door to Dane's room was also slightly opened and Ren caught a glimpse of dark decor, including what appeared to be high quality, black sheets making up the king sized bed. Her stomach flipped and she averted her eyes quickly, embarrassed by the scorching images that crossed her mind without any warning. When she looked up, she was trapped in his searing gaze; it conveyed a message without a single spoken word, the appropriate response to the naughty thoughts running through her head.

~

Damnit. It was Kerri who had run into him but with Ren this close to his room, all he could think about was drawing her inside and shutting the door behind him so they could lose themselves in bliss. He could envision her thick hair sliding across the Egyptian cotton sheets, her eyes closed, her mouth half open, the little sounds she would make, and the louder, more primitive sounds he would coax out of her. His heart rate hastened at the mere thought of it and he reached by her to pull the door shut quickly. He'd start behaving like an animal if he didn't check himself.

Ren cleared her throat, breaking the eye contact with Dane and put a hand on Kerri's shoulder. "Why don't you go check on Gage, while I talk to Dane about the daily grind of things here?"

Kerri nodded and took off up the stairs, leaving the pair alone. Ren jerked almost imperceptibly when Dane closed his hand around her elbow to guide her toward the kitchen. His fingers touched the translucent flesh in the crook of her arm, and he watched her from the corner of his eye, amused as gooseflesh rose on her skin. As much as he told himself he needed to restrain, he couldn't resist looking for these little reactions. It meant he wasn't alone. She took a couple of steps to get ahead of him to the kitchen and seated herself at the table, letting out a nervous breath.

Dane sat opposite her and slid the offer of employment document across the table to her.

"The job is pretty basic." He leaned back in his chair. "I think you probably get the general gist of taking care of kids."

She laughed as she scribbled her signature across the informal letter.

"I guess you could say that."

"Basically, just add Gage to that roster. Treat

the house like you would treat your own, come and go as you please. You have access to the sedan, I normally drive the truck."

She raised a brow and he groaned inwardly. He had known that Jimmy would be a point of contention.

"Trust me, it's easier on gas, and quite frankly... safer." He didn't want to put it into words, but he was essentially saying he didn't want Gage in that discreetly disguised deathtrap. The car had to have been at least as old as Ren. "Just park the Jimmy and use the car. Does that thing even have air conditioning?"

Her indignant expression gave him his answer. She twisted the pen between her fingers. "Bob has been with me for a long time."

"Bob?" Dane laughed out loud. The mood lightened and he was grateful. It was harder to think about the way his name would sound coming out of her mouth in the throes of ecstasy when he was considering she was *that* girl—the one who named her car.

She lifted her chin in playful defiance. "He's been a very important guy in my life. He needed a name. Jimmy Bob. Bob for short."

"Okay, well... *Bob* can take a hiatus. The cargo you'll be hauling around is pretty precious to me, and I suspect Kerri is the same to you, so we're going with safe, reliable vehicles."

"Bob got me here from the East coast, thankyouverymuch."

"Barely."

She smiled and he knew he'd won.

"Barely," she said.

"And while we're on the topic of Kerri, I have no problems with her giving you a hand with Gage. As long as he's staying out of trouble." He made a mental note to check with his mother about a couple of hours a week at the store for Kerri, to make her own pocket change.

"I think between the pair of us, we can probably manage. I mean, he's just a little boy, after all."

"Don't let the sweet little boy act trick you. That kid is sneaky—take your eyes off of him for two seconds and he's... well, he's falling off of corral panels and breaking his arm." Dane laughed, because with a few days between him and the accident, and a kid who was completely back to normal except for the fiberglass cast, that's all he could do. "Would you like to see the rest of the property?"

"Sure. I'll get the kids." Ren rose and called for Kerri and Gage from the bottom of the stairs. They barreled down like a herd of elephants, nearly landing in a heap at the bottom, followed closely by Rex who was never one to miss out on any excitement. "Dane and Gage are going to give us a tour of the ranch, Ker. Sound good?"

The four of them put on boots and headed out into the yard. The ranch settlement consisted several barns of varying sizes, a rough cabin and a number of small outbuildings. The property steadily inclined behind the barns and as far as the eye could see to the mountainous horizon was pasture, some of it dotted with livestock. In addition to the buildings, a long rectangular corral was situated with a short fence and then a round corral about sixty feet across with a much taller fence, perhaps six feet at its height, between the house and the barn.

Dane led them into the first barn, which housed several horses, who hung their heads out over the doors of their stalls, nickering amiably at their master as he passed. Each one had its ears pricked forward and looked genuinely pleased to see him. Here and there, Dane paused to stroke a nose or murmur a word of praise or warning to the horses. This barn housed the personal horses of the ranch, and Dane spent a lot of time here. If there was ever anything eating at him, even in the middle of the night, he'd find himself sitting on a bale of hay and listening to the horses' soft noises as they shifted and snoozed. There was an old adage that the outside of a horse was good for the inside of a man and Dane couldn't argue with it.

Kerri was instantly riveted by a gray head poking out over the top of a stall. Long, shapely ears led down to intelligent looking globes for eyes and a velvety soft looking muzzle. An expanse of forelock and mane hung into the horse's eyes and Kerri immediately moved to brush it away. While the rest of the group carried on, she lingered until Dane noticed she was no longer with the group. She was still at the gray, stroking its nose and murmuring baby words to the horse.

"Ah, this is Buckshot. He loves new friends." Dane approached and the horse turned his attention from the girl to the master. As soon as Dane reached out and stroked the gelding's forehead, he turned back to Kerri, clearly favoring the much more complete and thorough adoration.

"He's one of my oldest buddies. He taught my little brother, Gavin, to ride." At the mention of Gavin's name, Dane paused for a moment, flooded with memories of his brother, legs hanging barely long enough down the horse's barrel to feel like much more than a mosquito perching on his back. He swallowed hard and slid his hand down Buckshot's forehead again, trying to bring himself back to the present.

"Do you still ride him?" Kerri asked.

Dane could hear a twinge of hope in her voice. He nodded. "I don't, but Gage rides him sometimes. He prefers his pony, Chessy, these days, so Buckshot's had a pretty lazy last couple of years."

Gage's head bobbed affirmatively. "She's not as far to fall!"

Kerri looked back at the horse wistfully and sighed. She was laying it on thick and Dane would have had to have been completely oblivious not to recognize where this was heading.

"Would you and your sister like to learn to ride, Kerri?" Dane asked. The girl perked visibly at the question, and her fingers tightened against Buckshot's mane in excitement; he'd hit his mark.

"Really? Yes! Can we, Ren?"

Ren's big smile told him she was as excited as

Kerri was. He, for one, couldn't wait to see her on a horse. These girls would fit in just fine.

SEVEN

BY THE TIME she had gotten Gage to bed and Kerri comfortably ensconced in her new accommodations, Ren's body was exhausted, but her mind was racing. She attempted to settle in for bed—it had been a long day with a lot of activity—but she couldn't quiet her thoughts, so after attempting to unwind, she got up and left her bedroom.

Dane was nowhere to be seen, so she took an opportunity to tip-toe through the house, looking at the various pieces of artwork and decor in the hallways until she found herself in the living room. A huge leather couch flanked one side of the room, and a large flat screen TV that looked like it hadn't seen much use perched on the opposite wall. A fireplace with a variety of family photos upon the mantel was the primary focal point of the room. She turned the TV on for company, muted, and wandered over to look at the collection of framed images.

Front and center was a photo of a toddler-aged Gage, sitting on the lap of a laughing couple. Ren picked it up for a closer look. The man was clearly related to Dane, with the same blond hair and stormy eyes both Dane and Ella had. The woman was pretty, with shoulder-length strawberry blond hair and a slight build like Gage.

"I was hoping you were still up." Dane's deep voice startled her and she turned to find him holding two bottles of beer. He was freshly showered and wore a white t-shirt and plaid lounge pants. "It'll be nice to have some company in this house after Gage's bedtime. Another adult to talk to."

He got closer and offered her one of the bottles, taking a pull from the one he kept. He inclined his head toward the photo.

"Gage's parents, Gavin and June."

"What happened?" It was rude to ask, not to mention none of her business. She was here to take care of the house and the boy, that was it, but the words slipped out before she could stop them.

"They wrecked their rig coming home from a rodeo in Denver a couple of years ago." Dane swallowed hard and took another pull of his beer. Ren could see his eyes were glossy with emotion.

"I'm so sorry." Ren's words were quick, sorry she had asked. She would have been as imposed upon if someone had asked about her mother. "So that's how you ended up with Gage?"

"Gavin named me in the will. I don't know if

he realized what he was asking. Best I can do is try not to mess things up too badly."

Ren knew that feeling all too well.

"Parenting when you aren't a parent can be a challenge, for sure."

"It's been tough. I feel like it's about to get easier." He offered her a gentle smile, and gestured to the couch. They sat, one on each end, facing the other. "On the topic of parenting when you're not a parent..."

It was only fair, Dane had bared his pain to her. Ren steeled herself with a deep breath.

"My dad passed ten years ago... my mother is... not fit." Her jaw tightened as she thought of the abuse—verbal, physical, emotional. It was a long time ago, but the anger still lay close to her heart. "She was difficult before dad died, but afterwards..." She stopped, shook her head.

Anita Maddock had been a tough mother, to begin with. Declan had always complimented her in their relationship, softening the blows of her own childhood lacking in love. She was uncompromising and demanding, but it had always seemed like it was out of love, and a desire to see the girls succeed. After her father had passed, Ren's mother had gone off the deep end. Her daughters were all she had left of him and instead of cherishing them because of it, she blamed them for her loss. Ren had gone headfirst down a flight of stairs at her mother's hands at least once. She'd stayed far longer than made any sense because she felt Kerri needed her mother. She'd put off college and moving into her own place so she could be the buffer between Kerri and Anita the way her father had been for her. She'd given up trying to understand why Anita hated them so much, and conceded instead to a life as a protector.

It was when she had caught her mother with Kerri locked in the garage, the door closed and the car running, that she had taken her sister and never looked back.

First, they'd moved to the other side of town, but Anita had followed them. Progressively, the distances had gotten longer and longer until Ren had finally packed everything up and said a prayer the Jimmy would make it on the 12 hour trip cross country. A couple hours outside of Three Rivers, she'd stopped for a local map and chosen the town from a handful of other small municipalities. They had no connections here, no reason to be here, no reason for Anita to suspect they were here.

Dane didn't press any further when Ren stopped talking. He set his beer aside, reached across the couch and drew her into his side with one arm.

Ren stiffened at first but the second she felt the warm closeness of his strong body, she relaxed, melted into his side, and rested her head on his chest. He ran his calloused fingers over her hair. She felt like she could relax, and stop the nagging fire of fear in her gut for just a minute. It felt like nothing could happen to her in his strong arms.

I'm in a different kind of trouble, now.

~

Dane wanted to kiss her. So badly he ached. He remembered the pain of loss he had experienced, saw the same kind of pain, and fear in her eyes. They weren't so different. They had both experienced loss, and they both had to deal with the trauma the best way they knew how. His best way had gotten easier today.

This certainly wasn't the first time it had crossed his mind how much easier life would be with a woman of the house. With the ranch and Gage keeping him occupied, his opportunities to expand his social circle had become limited. He'd always thought he would have lots of time to settle down, but the accident had changed the course of his life in a way he would have never predicted. Now he had little time to develop any kind of relationship, that is, if a woman wasn't scared off by the ready-made family to begin with. He'd grown up with most of the women who still resided in Three Rivers and while many of them made a big show of how sexy a man with a kid was, when it came down to the nitty gritty, nobody wanted to be the mother of a child who wasn't theirs.

Right now, he was holding a woman who didn't seem scared of much, least of all a five year old boy and his uncle. Sure, she was his employee, but already he could see the tender way she interacted with Gage. She had more ease with the boy right off the bat than he could have wished for. If he couldn't have his mother, Ren seemed like she could be the next best thing.

She rested quietly, her breathing soft and even. He thought she may even have dozed off. It was comfortable, and they sat that way for some time, his thumb tracing gentle circles on her exposed bicep as he considered the twists and turns that had brought him to this juncture in his life, hiring a woman to play the role of someone he had been unsuccessful in finding the traditional way.

He'd always been a good uncle. He'd been busy learning the business side of the ranch when Gage was born and he'd lived vicariously through the little family. Gavin was made for fatherhood. The jury was still out on Dane, but he was trying his best.

He'd taken his role seriously when the accident happened, though the whole family had been pitching in since. Many times, Ella had offered to take Gage to live with them in town but there had been so much change for the child that Dane couldn't bear to make him leave the place he had grown up in. Who was he to disrupt the memories Gage might still cling to of his mother and father teaching him to ride, packing him in front of the saddle when they checked cattle, and gathering around the dining room table in this very house? The truth was, this new role was difficult. He was still Uncle Dane but he was also now in a position of fatherhood in addition to all of the roles he played before, and the balance was a challenge.

He heard thumping coming down the stairs and Ren jerked upright, leaping away from him as though she'd been shocked, and nearly spilling her beer. So she wasn't asleep after all. Kerri's head poked around the door frame, taking in the scene with a bemused expression. The girl was young but she wasn't an idiot.

"Do you know where the charger for my mp3 player is?" she asked Ren.

The older sister jumped to her feet just a little too quick, setting her beer on the side table and turning to Dane.

"I think I'm just going to head up for bed now, anyways... thanks for the beer and... conversation."

She scampered away and up the stairs, leaving Dane still reclined on the couch, his arm across the back where she had been sitting. He watched her shapely figure disappear up the stairs and his eyes lingered there for a moment longer.

As her employer, he knew he had to tamp down the feelings and urges he had about this girl, but as a man, he was struggling. Had he made a mistake hiring her? Probably. Would it look bad from the outside? Most likely. Did he care? Hell no.

EIGHT

DANE STOOD IN the doorway between the kitchen and hallway quietly, entertained by watching Ren. She'd opened the cupboard to the left of the sink twice, clearly looking for something, but this time, she stopped, as if taking inventory of what was inside and committing it to memory. The house *was* large and entirely foreign to her; he couldn't blame her—he forgot where things were half the time.

After watching her struggle for a second more—she was so damn cute doing it and he didn't mind the view when she stood on her tiptoes to peer into the higher cupboards—he cleared his throat and entered the kitchen.

"Whatcha looking for?"

She looked a little embarrassed and turned, offering him a bewildered smile.

"Cheese grater?"

He reached past her, second cupboard to the

left, passing so close the space between them shared their breaths, and produced the grater, one corner of his lips turned up in a mischievous grin.

"Lucky guess," he said.

She ducked her eyes for a moment but then met his again with a full-watt smile and his heart soared. The woman was attractive, he would give her that, but she also had a way of making him feel like the most important person on the planet when she cast her smile at him.

"I'm just trying to figure out the lay of the land. It's a big house."

He chuckled; she was right. The house felt particularly large and lonely when he was up after Gage went to bed. It was accustomed to being full-to-overflowing but the most action it usually saw these days was two Sundays a month, when everyone came over and Ella cooked a big meal while they caught up on anything that had been neglected for want of a few extra pairs of hands.

"That's the truth. You'll get used to it eventually." He took a step back, pushed his hands into his pockets for fear he'd reach out and touch the girl. He'd been thinking about the feel of her soft body against his as it had relaxed into his touch two nights ago. Not constantly, but every once in a while, when he wasn't paying attention, she'd cross his mind. She'd been here all of two days but that was all the time it had taken for him to know she was the kind of girl he could probably hold for a lifetime.

Her appealing feminine form wasn't the only

thing he could appreciate and she'd made that abundantly clear over the last couple of days. She was endlessly patient and kind with Gage, encompassing a maternal quality he wouldn't have expected in a childless woman of her age. Already, she had forged a great relationship with him, and she guided Kerri as if it was her second nature to parent a teenager. She could make just about any meal with any type of ingredients and for not having had a rural upbringing, she wasn't afraid of the fresh produce and meat Ella had delivered for them. In fact, he wasn't sure she was afraid of anything, least of all, hard work. Just this morning, he had caught her on her knees in his mother's long-abandoned and grown over garden, pulling weeds while Kerri listened to music on the porch and Gage played with the dog in the yard. She'd already made herself completely indispensable. He hadn't known how badly he needed someone like Ren in the house until she'd actually gotten there and shown him what he'd been missing for the last two years.

He wanted to know everything about her, from the finite details of what had happened with her mother, to her favorite color, right down to the noises she would make when he pressed his lips to the soft flesh of her throat.

In order to stop himself from finding out all of those things right now, he crossed the floor and pulled open the fridge, making a face at the contents.

"Looks like we need a grocery run. I've got to

drop Gage off at mama's for his weekly sleepover...
how about you, Kerri and I run into town?"

She pursed her lips like she had to think
about it.

"I'm fine to run into town alone. I'm sure
you're too busy to babysit me." When he arched a
skeptical brow at her, she conceded. "... but if you
have to go in anyways... I just don't want to be a
bother."

"It's no bother, trust me."

~

Twenty minutes later, Ren found herself in
the front seat of Dane's pickup, Kerri and Gage
buckled in safely behind. Gage chattered happily to
Kerri, telling her about how he ran Grandma's store
in return for supper and a sleepover once a week.

"So what do they sell there?" Kerri asked from
the back seat.

Dane met her eyes in the rear view mirror.
"Everything from a ladies' fart to a clap of thunder."

Ren turned to catch the absurd expression on
Kerri's face and laughed out loud. They were both
still figuring out the interesting, and oftentimes
amusing local dialect. Kerri struggled a bit more
though.

They stopped briefly at Baylor's store, Ella
waving at Ren and Kerri from the front door as
Gage skipped from the truck to his grandma. A five
minute drive past the store brought them to Three
Rivers' one independently owned grocery store.

The three disembarked from the truck and Dane gestured to the diner next door to the shop. A crowd of young people were congregated outside.

"They make a mean milkshake, Kerri, if you're not interested in groceries. Might be nice to meet some new faces?" The teen skipped off with a word of thanks and a five dollar bill from Ren, leaving her alone with Dane at the entrance of Sawyer's Grocery. He stepped ahead of her and pulled a shopping cart from the row, pushing it into the store.

Ren had scrawled a list on a sticky note and followed beside the cart, pulling items off of shelves and out of coolers as they moved slowly up and down each aisle so she could figure out where everything was.

"Eventually I'll know where everything is, but I'll still go up and down every aisle when I'm just here for a carton of eggs." Ren laughed.

"No, the eggs you'll get from the Pierces. You'll be here for cheese. We don't have a neighbor who makes that yet." To illustrate his point, Dane stopped and put a block of cheddar cheese into the cart—it hadn't been on Ren's list.

"Ah, gotcha." She made a mental note to figure out where the Pierces lived and pulled her list out to cross eggs off of it.

They continued down the aisles, taking their time - the banter between them was comfortable and easy.

Dane was a popular man. Just about everybody who passed by them stopped to say hello and was just as pleased to see Ren as they were to see him. Everyone knew he'd been raising Gage and were pleased to see he'd gotten some help. The Baylors were obviously well respected within the community and Dane was friendly, asking after grandkids and jobs. Ren had never had that kind of connection within a neighborhood and it made her heart ache a little bit.

As they made their way through the bakery, a short, white haired woman in a motor scooter nearly ran Ren over. Dane saw her coming and tugged Ren briefly to him, out of the line of fire. The woman's face lit up at the sight of Dane. He shot a good humored smile at Ren, murmuring, "Watch this."

"Dane Baylor! You grow taller every time I see you!" The woman flashed a smile at Dane that was full of adoration.

"I think you're just getting shorter, Mrs. Bates." He teased, his tone affectionate.

"And this, is this your new bride I have been hearing so much about?" The woman grasped Ren's hand. Ren smiled and patted the woman's hand lightly, completely confused. Her stomach did a flip-flop. This was either something bad or she was either the butt of a cruel joke.

"Oh Mrs. Bates... this is Ren Maddock, she works for me."

"I heard it was a beautiful wedding! I bet you've got a bun in the oven already. Have to catch up to Gavin. I've got to get going, Henry is waiting for me!"

Dane watched her go with an amused expression on his face. Ren shook her head at Mrs. Bates' back, flabbergasted at the way the woman had bowled the pair of them over.

"Have you been telling the locals you mail-ordered a bride?" she teased, recovering quickly.

"Mrs. Bates... I've known her my whole life and then some. She confuses me for Finn on a regular basis... she's done it ever since we were kids."

"Wait," Ren stopped, narrowing her eyes at Dane. Finn had sat at her dinner table the last two nights, but on his own. "Finn is married? Or is that completely imagined?"

"Was." Dane cleared his throat, continuing to push the cart through bakery without making eye contact. "Finn and Sunny were married all of six months when she was diagnosed with cancer. It went quick. That was about a year ago."

A curse escaped under Ren's breath. It was no wonder this family was so close. Two devastating strikes in the last two years, and those were just the ones he had disclosed to her. Who knew what else had happened—for all she knew, Dane was a widower, too. It put her issues into perspective— what business did she have complaining about her mother's presence in her life? At least she and Kerri were both still alive.

"I'm so sorry, Dane."

He shook his head, pushed the cart ahead and plucked a bag of Doritos off the shelf.

"Bad things happen to good people. It's part

of the journey. Gotta be there to get here."

She considered his words.

"That's a good way to look at it."

"It's the only way *to* look at it if you wanna make it through."

The rest of the shopping trip passed in general silence, but Ren had a deeper appreciation for the man who walked beside her. Not only did they have to deal with the grief of loss in their family, they regularly had well-meaning neighbors who couldn't keep things straight and dredged up the pain without intending to.

As they exited Sawyer's, grocery bags in hand, Ren caught sight of Kerri outside the restaurant. She was leaning against a wall with her back turned and a tall, gangly teen aged boy stood beside her, the pair of them peering down at her cell phone. Neither heard Ren and Dane approaching.

"And when you get home, go to the bathroom and lift your shirt and send me a picture of your tits..."

Ren stopped short, seeing red. She reached for the boy but Dane got there first, dropping his bag of groceries and clamping a hand on the boy's shoulder to turn him around and get a look at his face.

"Kyle Sullivan, I *know* your mama didn't teach you it was okay to talk to ladies like that."

The boy's eyes widened when he saw Dane's furious face. Dane pushed the kid a couple of steps back, hand still tight on his shoulder, until he was pressed against the brick wall of the restaurant. He wasn't overly rough but there was no give in his eyes. His voice was firm, his gaze pinning the boy's.

"You're gonna leave this girl alone. She's gonna take your number right out of her phone and you're not going to get *any* pictures of her, or of any other girl... 'cause you're not going to ask any girls for that kind of thing again."

Kerri's eyes remained rapt on the scene unfolding as Kyle nodded, giving Ren an opportunity to pull the phone from her sister's hand and hit the delete button on the contact she had been keying in. Kerri still hadn't moved when Ren put the phone back into her hand, but a bright blush had run up her fair cheeks and her eyes had filled with embarrassing tears. Ren put her arm around her sister's shoulders and squeezed reassuringly.

Though Kyle clearly didn't feel he should have to, a sullen apology crossed his lips.

"I'm sorry, Dane."

"Don't you think you should be telling *Kerri*, here, that you're sorry for disrespecting her?" Dane didn't hesitate to correct the boy.

"I'm sorry for disrespecting you, Kerri." The boy didn't lift his eyes to either of the recipients of his apology, and shuffled back to a crowd of young people who had gathered to watch the altercation. Some of them jeered at Kyle for being schooled by an 'old guy', others slapped him on the back in congratulations.

Dane glared at the group and then turned, putting a hand on Kerri's shoulder as he picked up his discarded grocery bags and guided the Maddock girls away from the diner.

"That kid is bad news, Kerri. I'm sorry," he said as the trio returned to Dane's pick-up. "I'll take you down to one of the rodeo nights sometime and introduce you to some good people."

Kerri shrugged, her strides matching theirs. The flush was still in her cheeks and her eyes were downcast. "It's okay."

It occurred to Ren, as she watched her sister, that she just expected people to treat her poorly. In truth, Ren had felt the same way for much of her adolescence. Being taken advantage of was normal and sincerity was rare and appreciated.

They were almost to the truck when Kerri spoke again, so quietly Ren almost didn't hear her. "Thanks, Dane."

"No thanks necessary. First thing's first. Nobody disrespects a woman, least of all when I'm there, and one I care about. Second of all, and trust me on this one - the only men worth knowing are cowboys. The Sullivans only ride gas-powered horses, and not a one of them has ever treated a lady right." He started off somber but by the time he finished and they were all piled in the truck, Dane's tone was teasing.

When they got back to the ranch, Kerri immediately headed for her bedroom and Dane helped Ren put the groceries away.

"Thanks for what you did for Kerri back there." Ren put the block of cheese in the fridge and straightened.

"It was nothing, really."

Leaning back against the counter, she took in his casual expression.

"I know it was nothing to you, but it was something to her. She's had a rough life, and someone besides me being kind to her is pretty monumental."

"Look, you girls are part of my family now." When Ren chuckled aloud, he continued. "Seriously. Wait until you meet the rest of my family. Nobody's just an employee. Everybody's family."

Considering all of the 'employees' she was currently aware of, Ren raised a skeptical brow at him and Dane raised his hands in mock surrender.

"Okay, currently, all the employees *are* family, literally. But you two have already made yourselves indispensable, so... family."

"Well... "

Dane cut her off with a raised finger.

"Family. Gage sees you that way already."

"Fine. Family."

Ren hoped she could remember the meaning of the word.

NINE

"ARE YOU *SURE* you've never been on a horse? You're doing awesome." Dane narrowed Kerri in his sights. She was sitting on Buckshot, as he had promised. She was clearly a little nervous but he was trying his best to make her more comfortable. Today was a day that reminded him how much better he was with horses than people.

Ever on his radar, Ren was riding Roxy nearby in small circles. He'd given her a quick rundown on brakes and steering and she was working out the mechanics of it all on her own. Though he'd done his best to persuade him to sit this one out, Gage trotted one handed around the whole lot of them on Chessy. Kerri, however, needed a little confidence booster. She was sitting hunched forward, having a hard time anticipating the movements of the horse.

Gage and Chessy lapped by Buckshot and the old horse's pace at the walk hastened just a half a step.

Kerri panicked. "Whoa!" Crumbling forward on herself, she grabbed the saddle horn and forgot about the reins. The horse immediately came to a stop. Ren pulled up to observe and Kerri's fearful eyes met Dane's.

"You told him to stop!" Gage called. He hadn't slowed even a bit in his trek around the ring.

"He's right. Buckshot's the kind of horse that's gonna take care of you. He felt you were off balance and when you said 'whoa', that was his signal to stop." Dane stepped forward, patted the horse's neck and then tapped Kerri's knee affectionately.

She straightened almost immediately, the knowledge that Buckshot wouldn't be galloping away with her hanging on desperately seemed to bolster her confidence.

"Give it another try, one more circle around the arena and then you two can help me feed."

Gage let out a celebratory whoop as Kerri nodded and squeezed her legs on the horse's side, giving him the signal to move forward. Dane took a few steps back to give her some space to turn, tucking his hands in his pockets.

For all Ren had told him about the last four years of their life, Kerri had turned out to be a pretty good kid. So far, she had proven to be respectful and polite. She was kind to Gage even if she still wasn't sure what to make of his blatant admiration for her. Every minute Dane spent with the Maddock girls made him believe he'd made the right choice to hire Ren and invite them into his home.

Ren steered Roxy toward Dane and came to a stop in front of him. He smiled up at her—she was a sight on a horse. She looked right at home up there. Maybe she wasn't an accomplished rider yet, but he'd make one of her, and there wasn't much sexier in his books than a good woman on a good horse. She was comfortable and not afraid and those were two of the more pressing factors in becoming a competent rider. He wondered if there was any challenge he could throw at her that she wouldn't meet bravely with a smile on her face.

"So. I have the brakes, gears and steering down so far. It's the dismount I'm not so sure about."

"Same as mounting up, just backwards." He chuckled.

"Except the potential to land on my ass is doubled." Her tone was sarcastic, but her face said she was teasing.

He approached, putting a hand on the horn of the saddle and standing parallel to the horse's side, creating a safe landing space for her.

"I won't let you fall on your ass. Now tip forward, swing your right leg over her rump and step down. I'll be right here to catch you."

She did as he told her, stepping down and a touch too far back. Losing her balance, she toppled backwards into him. He drew a sharp breath at the feel of her whole body pressed against him and she took an abrupt step forward to right herself as if she'd backed into a hot wood stove. He had made an effort not to touch her, not even a casual brush, since the night he'd held her on the couch, and it was like electricity coursing through him when they made contact just now. She took a moment to turn around - she felt it, too.

Goddamn, but she was like a magnet. He wanted to be close to her, to touch her. He realized too late that he was standing too close for comfort, mere inches between his body and hers, and finally stepped back, not without effort, clearing his throat.

"Told you I wouldn't let you fall on your ass." His teasing tone cut the tension crackling through the air and lightened the mood. He slipped the leather reins over Roxy's head and handed them to Ren. "Now you get to learn how to untack. There's no falling involved in that part."

~

So maybe she hadn't fallen on her ass, Ren thought, but she was clearly falling for this man. Mere days into her employment at the Baylor Ranch and she was already longing to put her hands on Dane Baylor's body, imagining what he would taste like, wondering what it would feel like when that storm his eyes kept promising came on.

She had the kitchen to herself since Dane had the kids feeding stock with him. A roast had been in the oven all afternoon while they'd been trying out the horses, and she busied herself with potatoes and carrots for the stove top, keeping watch out the kitchen window for the trio she was beginning to feel was her little family.

Though she told herself the reason she shouldn't feel anything at all for Dane was because he was her employer and she was his employee, it went so much deeper. Setting down any kind of real tie in Three Rivers meant that when the inevitable happened, and Anita found them, the departure would be much more complicated, that much more painful. Ren had just about had it with unnecessary pain.

She sighed, putting the finishing touches on gravy from the roast drippings as she heard Dane, Kerri and Gage come tramping up the steps, laughing and chattering. Dane took off his hat and swatted Gage playfully on the behind.

"You two go wash up for dinner, you smell like you were playing in the manure pile."

Gage wiggled his bottom cheekily in the door of the kitchen and scooted forward with a squeal towards the bathroom when Dane stomped playfully toward him as if to swat him again.

When the kids left, he settled himself with his hips against the counter, watching her for a moment. As far as Ren was concerned, he was always too close. Being in the same house was too close. She was always acutely aware of his presence, his proximity to her. The only relief she had was when he was out in the barns, and she hoped, as she settled into her role, that would be more frequent.

Now she could feel not only his presence but

his eyes on her as she stirred the gravy. Finally, she looked up and met his gaze. She couldn't spend her whole life skittering away from him or frozen with a racing heart.

"What are you doing this weekend?" The smile on his face gave away his intentions.

She cocked her head, narrowing her eyes at him.

"I don't know, but I have a feeling you're about to tell me." She turned the heat on the stove down and wiped her hands on a dish towel.

"How'd you know?" He chuckled.

"You're the boss." Her tone teased but she hoped it got the point across. He was only deterred for a moment.

"I'd like to take you to the dance hall on Friday. Give you a chance to meet some folks, get a feel for the community. Have a little bit of fun."

Despite her resolve to feel nothing, a whole mess of butterflies took flight in the pit of Ren's stomach. She gave him a dubious look.

"Do I have a choice in the matter?" It wasn't that she didn't want to spend an evening dancing with him. It was that this was more unnecessary pain—spending time with him outside of her employment, giving herself a taste of what she knew she couldn't have.

"I'm the boss." He tipped his head with a playful smirk. His teasing manner and good mood were infectious and she found a small smile slanting the corner of her lips.

"Okay, okay. What about the kids?"

"Mama will come take care of them for the evening." He eyed her again, took his hat in both hands. "I can see you are skeptical about this plan. Trust me. You're going to have a blast."

TEN

REN NERVOUSLY SMOOTHED down the front of her sun dress. She'd bought it on one of her evenings off this week with Kerri's help because she knew her huge closet needed a dress in it but she'd also let herself imagine what it would be like to wear it for *him*. It was a delicate cream eyelet lace pattern that hit just above her knees with a sweetheart bodice and halter top. It was really not something she'd normally wear but by the expression on her sister's face when she'd come out of the dressing room along with her own surprise when she looked in the full length mirror, she knew it was coming home with her.

Kerri had been a little dismayed not to have been invited but Dane had graciously offered to take her to a local rodeo day the next weekend so she could meet some of the kids she'd be attending school with in the fall. She'd helped Ren get ready, suggesting makeup techniques and helping coax her normally wavy auburn hair into sultry curls. Ella had stopped by not five minutes before and taken the kids to get take out for dinner at a local restaurant, leaving Ren alone in her room to put the finishing touches on her outfit and her courage.

Since the night they'd talked about their families, she had tried to keep her distance. In those moments, they had become familiar—too familiar, and she felt with the physical barrier broken between them, nothing good could follow. Nothing that would let her keep her job and fly under her mother's radar, anyways.

Oh, but she wanted him. She released a long breath, letting her mind wander to the incredible specimen that was her employer. The body that wouldn't quit, the tough exterior that encased a heart of gold. He wasn't accustomed to showing it but she could see it when he interacted with Gage, when he had held her that night in the living room. It had been a long time since she'd been held like that, and longer still since she'd felt a sense of relief and comfort, like her life was finally on track.

Her train of thought was disrupted by a soft knock. She looked up to see Dane standing in the partially open door, an expression on his face she couldn't quite read. He was wearing a pair of dark denim jeans that fit just right, a pair of boots that clearly hadn't seen as much dust as the ones he wore day to day, a long sleeved, black button down shirt with the sleeves rolled a third of the way up and a clean, crisp white Stetson.

"You look beautiful, Ren." His words were

reverent and sincere, and a blush rose in her cheeks. She had heard as many cruel comments as kind about her body. She had a little too much padding here and there, just enough to get the 'lose 15 pounds and you'd be a stunner' comments. Between working to take care of Kerri financially and actually taking care of Kerri, 15 pounds was a nemesis she hadn't had a chance to take down. She offered Dane a faulty smile, breaking eye contact and looking down. She wanted to say thank you but it was difficult not to brush the compliment off, so she didn't dare open her mouth.

He crossed the room to her in a few short steps, breaking the physical barrier that had laid between them for the last few days and tipped her chin up to meet his gaze, a soft smile lighting his features, his eyes serious.

"I mean it."

She pursed her lips, searching his eyes. This man had no reason to lie to her. She found the words.

"Thank you."

~

The dance hall was crowded and loud, the way Dane liked it. The people of Three Rivers convened here often, setting aside whatever differences might have plagued them through the week, to let loose and have a couple of beers. It had been a while since Dane had been able to get here and people noticed.

Poor Ren looked overwhelmed by the raucous gathering. He casually slid an arm around her waist to keep her from getting lost in the sea of people as they cut across the back end of the dance floor to the bar. A couple of his regular dance partners took note, cocking an eyebrow. Dane had always been the sort of man who didn't turn down a spin on the dance floor—and he was making a bold statement now, by arriving with a woman and making a physical claim on her. He knew his offers to dance tonight would be few and far between, but he had a sincere hope the smoking hot siren on his arm would fill the position.

At the very least, she hadn't shied away from his arm around her waist and it made his heart swell up with pride. She was a beautiful woman and he was pleased she allowed him to get close to her. He had nearly swallowed his tongue when he'd seen her in that dress and the other men in the dance hall had noticed it too. Fitted in all the right spots, it accentuated the curves of her body and offset the dramatic auburn of her hair. At this proximity, he could smell the delectable scent of honey and sunflowers wafting off her pale skin.

With the noise so overpowering in the hall, any conversations were done in close quarters, and Dane tipped his head to speak directly into Ren's ear. Close enough to take in the enticing smell of her, he imagined pressing his lips to the soft hollow behind her ear, tasting the sweetness of her skin as his teeth nicked her earlobe playfully. He took a moment to convince himself not to drag her into the nearest dark corner and devour her.

"What are you drinking?"

Under his hand, he felt Ren take in a slow breath and release it carefully before she turned her head to position her own mouth near his ear and speak.

"Rye and ginger ale? It's been so long since I've had a drink."

A noisy trio of young man jostled into Ren then, pushing her body against him as they headed for the bar. Dane didn't have to speak, just directed a sharp glare to draw an apology from the group. He moved his other arm around Ren protectively to steady her and then released her quickly, before it became a mistake he wanted to make and he dragged her against his body in front of God and a third of the residents of Three Rivers.

"You wait here, the bar is crazy." And it was— it was where the boys who'd pushed her had been heading, and people were crushing in toward the bartenders. The people of Three Rivers enjoyed their alcoholic indulgences when it came to social gatherings. He parked her near a pillar and left to cut his way through the crowd.

Cutter Anderson was tending the bar and he smiled when he saw Dane approach. They had graduated together and like Dane, Cutter had never left Three Rivers. Some of them just didn't have the thirst for the big city, and as far as he knew, the Andersons were going through a struggle with their ranch. Cutter stayed close to support his family with whatever additional odd jobs he could pick up.

"Hey Baylor, what can I get for you?"

Leaning one elbow on the bar, Dane ordered. "Rye and ginger and my regular."

Cutter raised a brow. "Rye and ginger, eh?"

"For the lady."

Tipping the spirits bottle into a Collins glass, the bartender eyeballed the measurements, added half a scoop of ice and filled the glass with ginger ale, sliding it across the bar.

"The lady, eh?"

"I know you want to ask, Anderson, get on with it." Dane took the bottle of beer his friend offered and popped the cap off.

"Who is she, where'd she come from and how long have you been tapping that? Also, am I invited to the wedding?"

Dane rolled his eyes and steeled himself with a pull from his bottle. From Cutter, he could tolerate a little bit of rudeness. The pair regularly hassled one another good-naturedly and this was par for the course.

"She's the homemaker I hired, she's here to schmooze with the good people of Three Rivers and *nobody* is 'tapping that', least of all me. I'm her boss." He said it as much to convince himself as his friend.

"No shit, so she's living at the house with you?"

Dane nodded, knowing what was coming next.

"Then you won't be the boss for long." Cutter made the noise of a whip cracking, winked at his friend, and headed down the bar to help the next person.

Shaking his head, Dane turned back to the dance floor and saw a small circle of people milling around Ren. He noticed a couple of friends of his mother's, no doubt offering help and casseroles. It didn't matter that she was an employee, what mattered was that she was a newcomer to town and they wanted to make her feel welcome. It was one of the many things he loved about the dusty town he'd called home his whole life. There was rarely a lack of hospitality.

He made his way back across the floor to her elbow, sliding into the conversation easily and offered Ren the drink.

"Oh hey, Mrs. Lawson here was just telling me about the time you kissed Jenny Benson on the playground and made her cry." There was a sparkle of mischief in Ren's eye and Dane liked it. "You don't make a habit of that, do you? Making girls cry?"

Dane rolled his eyes and took another swig of his beer.

"Mrs. Lawson, you shouldn't be sharing all my secrets. Ren might think I'm a scoundrel."

Ren shrugged innocently. "No comment."

ELEVEN

REN HAD BEEN passed around the dance floor a dozen times. The first dance with Dane had been upbeat and was a distant memory since it felt like she'd had a new partner for every song, including every neighboring rancher, and the remainder of the Baylor boys. Right now, the patriarch of the Baylor family had made an appearance and Caine was swinging her around the room like it was nothing.

She couldn't say she wasn't relieved when she felt a tap on her shoulder and turned to see Dane with what was her third or fourth drink from the bar in hand, along with a bottle of water.

"I'm just gonna cut in here, dad."

"I suppose I ought to head home to your mother. She kicked me out for some quality one on one with the kids." Caine laughed.

He thanked Ren for the dance and headed for the door, leaving her with Dane. They were surrounded by people but she felt like they were the only two in the room, the way he seemed to narrow her in his sights. He guided her toward one of the vacant tables.

"You having a good time?"

Ren nodded eagerly, the drink lowered many of her inhibitions and she'd given herself up to having a good time. The joyous mood in the dance hall was infectious, and everyone was friendly and warm.

"I am. Your dad is tireless."

"He makes *me* feel like an old man, sometimes." Dane laughed.

Toying with the straw in her drink, Ren looked up at Dane. She'd barely seen him since the first neighbor had cut in to ask for a dance. She didn't have any right to wonder what he'd been doing or who he'd been passing the time with, but she felt a hot stab of jealousy at the idea of him spinning another woman around the dance floor. She wanted to ask but he perked as the pretty strains of a slow acoustic country song came over the speakers.

He tipped his head, one corner of his lips slanted up in a devilish smile that brought out a dimple.

"I think it's my turn for another dance."

She feigned reluctance for just a moment but finished off the last sip of her drink and took his hand as he guided her toward the dance floor.

Dane took her into his arms with the same comfort and ease that pulled her to his side the first night she'd spent in his home. She put her arms around his neck as he folded her up into his embrace, holding her closer than might have been appropriate for their relationship but it felt just right to her. The alcohol had warmed her insides and the closeness tipped her over the boiling edge as he began to lead their bodies in a gentle sway.

Ren knew she could give herself up to this, let go and stop resisting, and hope the chips fell in her favor. It might have been the alcohol talking but for a few moments in his arms, she could imagine the four of them as a family with one on the way. Smart girls didn't fall for the far-fetched happily ever after. They didn't fall for the white knight in the form of a tall, handsome cowboy, and they certainly didn't fall for their boss. Ren didn't feel like a very smart girl tonight.

One of Dane's hands had settled on the small of her back, the other slid easily up her spine, under her thick fall of hair, his fingertips landing lightly on the nape of her neck, and drawing goosebumps from her flesh. She met his eyes, shaken out of her moment of imagination and took in a shuddering breath as she realized how focused, how hot his gaze on her was. With a tiny bit of pressure, he tipped her head back and covered her mouth with his.

The kiss felt like falling. It felt like relief. She made the softest noise of surrender. At that, Dane pulled back, his eyes conveying the question, asking for forgiveness for what had transpired and forgiveness for what would happen next. Her response was to pull him closer, joining their mouths once again. The first taste was addictive.

He teased his tongue across the seam of her lips and she opened to him willingly. Maybe it was the alcohol or the heat in the crowded dance hall, the lazily seductive thrum of the baseline in the music, or maybe it was because she allowed herself to want him. He stroked the inside of her mouth, probing lightly, tasting her tentatively.

If people were watching, she didn't notice. She was completely wrapped up in the moment and feel of him so close to her. Their swaying slowed and eventually stopped as he used the hand on the small of her back to press her body tightly to his. The way he clutched her tight to his chest drove any doubts she had about his desires out of her mind. She was not accustomed to being wanted and the feel of his hard body against hers turned her insides to pure molten.

She was breathless when Dane finally pulled away, his slate eyes fiery. It was a demanding, devouring side of him she hadn't yet seen. Without a word, he put a hand on her waist and guided them out of the dance hall. Her heart racing with anticipation, she paid no attention to the handful of people sober enough to take notice of the show they had been putting on in the middle of the dance floor.

They barely made it back to the truck before the kiss picked up where it had left off, making good on the promises Dane's eyes had made. Ren had no time to object before his mouth came sweeping down, hot over hers. It took away her breath and her reason. In this close proximity, with his mouth claiming hers, she couldn't remember or imagine why she would have ever wanted to say no to this man.

He didn't break the kiss as he reached out to lower the tail gate of the truck and turned their bodies. His hands on her waist lifted her effortlessly to perch her up on it. He nudged her knees apart to make a perfect v to cradle his body close to hers. Instinctively, Ren tightened her knees around his hips, drawing him in. The noise he made into her mouth when their bodies came flush nearly undid her. A hot stone of desire built in the pit of her stomach as she shamelessly pressed herself to him, feeling his arousal, hard muscle under her fingers, the manliness of him; all of the things she had been thinking of for days.

Finally breaking the kiss, he let his mouth wander liberally across her jaw, to the sensitive skin of her throat where he paused, sucking briefly. While one hand loosely cradled her jaw, the other slid down her back and pressed her tighter to him, the skirt of her sun dress sliding up her thighs slowly. Her nerves were so awake even the slide of fabric against her skin made her ache to imagine how his hands might feel doing the same thing.

The truck had been backed into a parking space against the wall, which provided them little privacy in the darkness, but Ren didn't care. It felt good, so good, to feel desire for someone, to feel them react with desire. She shuddered as his hand moved from the small of her back to her bare knee, his calloused fingers providing just the right amount of friction as they slid upwards, upwards, until he was cupping her hip under the skirt of her dress. If she hadn't been so lost to the feel of his mouth, his breath, his hands on her, she might have thought of the indecency of it, but she was bobbing out of control on the rough waters of desire.

He slid his hand down, his thumb hitching under the leg band of her panties as his mouth found hers again, tugging lightly at her lower lip as he finally made contact with her core. Ren gasped as his fingers found purchase, gripping his shoulders tightly as he moved in a lazy, light circle around the most sensitive part of her.

"Oh God!" She rasped out. Shamelessly, she pushed her hips forward, further, closer to him. His light touch made her blood sing but it wasn't enough. He let out a tight breath against the sensitive flesh of her neck, and followed it with a light nip.

"Easy, sugar. Make it last."

His words nearly undid her, his achingly slow pace whipping her into frenzy. It was like he was guiding her up a mountain and she knew when she reached the precipice, she would fly. She gripped his shoulders tighter with one hand, panting in his ear as her other hand tightened in his hair.

She whimpered as she neared the first good orgasm she'd had in ages.

"Shhh." He held her against his chest, his lips against her temple, his pace steady but unyielding as he drove her body toward ecstasy. "I've got you, Ren, don't worry."

He tipped her over the edge with the lightest of touches and she shuddered in his grip. Biting back a feral cry, she pressed her face to his shoulder, sobbing with pleasure. He soothed her, one hand tracing a gentle path from her bare shoulders down to her bottom and up again.

When she'd had a moment to pull herself together, she straightened, reaching for him. Tipping her chin up, Dane pressed a chaste kiss to her lips and smiled.

"It's getting late, I ought to get you home."

"Wait..."

He leaned in close, his hot breath tickling her ear.

"Trust me, there isn't much I want to do more than lay you out in the bed of this truck and make love to you until the sun comes up. But this isn't the place, and you need time." He backed up, sliding her off of the tailgate until she was on her feet but didn't let go of her.

She meant to be indignant about his words but he had a point. She straightened her dress, smoothing it down in much the same way she had earlier that evening. They moved around the side of the truck and he helped her into the passenger seat, leaning in to press a heated kiss to her lips before he shut the door carefully and passed in front of the hood to get in the driver's seat.

The drive back to the Baylor ranch passed in silence. Ren was hard pressed to keep her eyes open as the alcohol and late hour caught up to her but Dane kept a steady undercurrent of pleasure thrumming through her body with his hand on her bare knee, his thumb stroking lightly as he guided the truck through the deserted streets of Three Rivers.

Most of the lights in the big house were out when they pulled in the driveway. Ella's car was parked in front of the porch and she met them in the kitchen, nursing a mug of coffee and reading a hardback novel.

Ren was self-conscious as they appeared in the doorway, tugging the hem of her dress down as far as she could get it. She felt like a teenager caught after a heavy make out session. Would Ella know what they had been up to? She twisted her fingers together nervously. *No, ma'am, I haven't been letting your son do sinful things to me in the dark.*

She peeked up over her reading glasses. "You kids have fun?"

"Of course. Thanks for keeping the kids, mama." Dane rounded the table and leaned over to give Ella a kiss on the cheek.

"Anytime, sweetheart. You know I never say no to spending time with Gage, and Kerri..." Ella shook her head. "You've done a fine job with that girl, Ren. She's as sweet as the day is long."

Ren smiled, grateful the conversation had steered away from the evening's events and to the kids.

"Thank you, Ella. I try my best. Teenagers

aren't always easy."

Ella laughed as she closed her book and rose from the table, looked pointedly at Dane.

"No, they aren't. At least you can reason with a girl. Boys give you heart palpitations every second day." She slid her arm around Dane's shoulders and gave him a squeeze. "I'll be taking off now, Caine is waiting up. He's a nervous Nellie, that one."

They bid Ella farewell and Ren went to pour herself a glass of water. She could feel Dane's presence behind her at the sink. Apparently, her self-consciousness hadn't worn off and she turned quickly, swallowing hard. The dance hall had been a different world altogether, but this was the house—their regular territory, where she was reminded that he was her boss and she had to protect the fragile life she was carving out here with Kerri.

"I think I'll head up to bed now." She put forth a delicate smile and edged away from him.

"Ren?"

She turned.

"I had a great time tonight."

Her smile was stronger this time. "Me too."

TWELVE

REN AWOKE WITH a start, her head pounding and her mouth dry. Glancing at the clock, she realized she had overslept by at least an hour and she leaped out of bed before her body and her mind could get their act together. She could hear voices from downstairs. Stumbling into the bathroom, she hurriedly brushed her teeth, and tugged her tangled hair into a ponytail high atop her head.

Taking the stairs two at a time, she hit the kitchen just in time to see Dane scooping scrambled eggs and bacon onto four plates. A bolt of desire shot through her a second before a wave of regret for the horrifying mistake she'd made the night before washed it well out to sea. She felt terrible—emotionally *and* physically, and she realized she was proving what a terrible choice she had been for this job.

She had wanted him to touch her, she had enjoyed every second of it. The alcohol she'd consumed had only made it easier to cast caution into the wind and accept what she had desired since she'd first laid eyes on Dane Baylor. A man had never touched her in such a masterful, easy way, clearly intent on her pleasure above anything else and asking nothing in return. Yes, she had wanted every second of what happened last night—still did—but she wasn't sure she could now live with the aftermath of it, the awkwardness... her own guilt.

Though she'd rushed away from him when they'd gotten home, Ren would have been lying if she said she hadn't tossed and turned for an hour trying to get to sleep with the feel of him a memory on her skin.

Dane looked up, smirked a bit at her appearance and gestured to an empty seat next to Gage. She blushed, remembering the wicked things those lips had done to her resolve the night before.

"Sit."

She started to protest but he shook his head resolutely and put a cup of coffee down at the place setting along with a couple of pain killers. Offering him a gracious smile, she sat and washed the pills down with a swig of coffee.

"I'm so sorry I overslept..."

"Don't be silly." Dane cast a look at the kids sitting opposite them. "Like I told the kids, the last week or so has been busy for you, you need to catch up on your rest."

"But the ranch... This is a job, not a vacation." He had better things to do than play Mr. Mom to Gage and especially Kerri, for whom she felt she should be the only one responsible.

"Noah has been staying at Finn's since you guys arrived, helping out with the stock. They figured I might want to help you get settled, learn the ropes... find your way around town."

His voice dipped imperceptibly with his last few words, tightening Ren's insides as she thought of what that had encompassed the night before. She let out a long breath. He had carried on as if it didn't mean a thing, but she knew it had been intentional.

How was she supposed to continue to work here while the thought of his rough hands on her skin shot through her mind at the mere sight of him? How was she supposed to focus on caring for his nephew when she couldn't stop thinking of the heat-laden tone of his voice when he'd called her *sugar*?

"Eat."

She took a deep breath and picked up her fork, working at the breakfast as her skeptical stomach allowed, trying to figure out just what she was going to do about the trouble she found herself in now.

The kids devoured their food in record time while Ren was still pushing the remains of her eggs around on the plate. Dane glanced at the wall clock and got up from the table.

"I *do* have to get out there now, though, the farrier is coming for the horses." He moved around the table and ruffled Gage's hair lightly. "Be good?"

The remaining trio busied themselves tidying

up the kitchen after breakfast. Dane's food had been excellent, but he wasn't exactly efficient when it came to minimizing the amount of dishes he dirtied. With the dishwasher loaded and everything put away, they headed to the yard for a game of hide and seek with Rex in tow.

After what had to have been the tenth round, with Ren doing most of the seeking, the girls had both run out of energy long before the boy and his dog. Kerri cornered her, looping her arm in Ren's and leaning conspiratorially close while they sat on the porch watching Gage and Rex running over the lawn.

"So. Was it dreamy?"

"What do you mean, was it dreamy?" Ren narrowed her eyes at her sister.

"I mean, did he kiss you? Was it romantic?" Kerri's earnest expression almost made Ren laugh out loud. If she had any idea... dreamy wasn't the word to describe it, and Ren was glad Kerri had no idea what the other options were.

"One: Dane is my boss. Two: I don't think that's any of your business, thankyouverymuch."

"Well, you always make *me* tell you what happened after I spend time with my friends. You just never went out with friends before so I never had a chance to make you tell me until now. So now you need to tell me." Kerri's tone was matter-of-fact.

"I danced with my *friend*, Dane. And I danced with Finn and Noah and Caine, too. And about half of the rest of the town, I couldn't keep track of their names."

The younger girl's face screwed up, frustrated. "But did he kiss you?"

Ren shot her sister down with a pointed look that invited no further conversation. Kerri was quieted for a moment, still leaning against her sister's shoulder as she watched Gage throw a stick for Rex. After a moment, she broke the silence.

"I'm not stupid, you know. You didn't say yes, but you didn't say no so you wouldn't have to lie to me."

"Kerri Ann Maddock, we are *not* having this conversation anymore." Her tone was not unkind as Ren released herself from her sister's hold and rose to her feet. "Time to wash up for a snack, guys."

Out of breath, Gage flopped down on the steps before her. "Help, I'm tired!"

Kerri rolled her eyes good-naturedly but helped the boy to his feet. "You're being silly."

Ushering everyone inside, Ren cursed silently. Her sister was perceptive and her burgeoning interest in men only magnified it. Kerri would never just let this drop. Ren had to figure out a way to put this to bed.

THIRTEEN

"SO LIFE IS a bit easier?" Finn Baylor rode alongside his brother, checking fences. The pair spent a lot of time on horseback, contemplating life. It was how they'd grown up and Dane imagined them this way until they were old and gray and not able to ride anymore. He'd come to understand his brother better than he understood just about anybody else through these rides, so he knew his brother's question was a bit more than loaded.

Dane considered his response before speaking. Easier in that he wasn't constantly wondering what Gage was getting into because he knew the boy was safe with a woman who cared for the child as though he was her own? Absolutely. Easier in terms of being able to focus on the ranch and not on the sweet, independent, thoughtful woman who was living in his house, and all the naughty things he'd like to do to her? Definitely not. And it was only worse now that he'd tasted her, tipped her over the edge and seen the expression of pure bliss as she'd found release.

Though he'd never been one to kiss and tell, Dane knew his brother wanted to know what happened after he and Ren left the dance floor so abruptly. Eighty percent of Three Rivers probably wanted to know. He hadn't intended to make such a show and it hadn't been right by any stretch of the imagination, but damnit, it felt right. And he deserved to have something good in his life.

"It is. Gage just loves her."

The safe bet. He should have known he'd find himself on the business end of an interrogation coming out here with Finn. Noah had been called into town to work the shop and he knew better than to leave Finn alone to ride fence—Dane would never have heard the end of it. He had a feeling he wasn't going to hear the end of it about the dance hall last night, either. *Damned if you do, damned if you don't.*

"I'm not sure he's the only one." Finn teased, reining in his horse and dismounting fluidly for a piece of fence that needed tightened. His horse snatched a mouthful of grass and stood by patiently.

"Shut up or you'll be walking back."

Dane wished he could have protected whatever it was that had been building with Ren, but they had thrown that idea into the wind when he couldn't keep his hands off of her on the dance floor.

"I guess that means you won't take too kindly

to me asking her out." Finn shot his brother a smirk. The Baylor brothers had shared many things over their lifetimes, but women were one of the things they had made a solemn pact not to.

Dane couldn't say he didn't wish things were a little different, that he didn't want Ren for himself so badly. Finn barely had time to come to terms with the diagnosis before they were laying Sunny in the ground. To hear him even *tease* about asking a girl out was the most interest he'd shown in a woman since he'd lost her. But here, Dane was going to be selfish. Ren was for him, nobody else, not even his grieving brother.

When his brother didn't answer immediately, Finn laughed. "That's all the answer I needed."

He finished twisting wires together and swung a leg over his horse's back, remounting with ease. Though all of the Baylor brothers had a way with horses, Finn was the one who looked like he was born to sit astride. He had a way of taking the most difficult horse and turning it into a soft, malleable partner. The pair turned a pretty good profit starting young colts but Finn also had a lucrative sideline working with those horses that were labeled as impossible, dangerous and worthless. In fact, the horse he rode now had come to the ranch not worth the steel nails his shoes were held on with. A couple of weeks with Finn Baylor had turned Jet into a formidable ranch horse with a strong bond to his trainer-turned-owner.

"That's the last one." Dane further avoided the questions about Ren and reined his horse around, aiming for the barns.

They rode back down to the homestead in relative silence, the only conversation that was safe for Dane was about the work that needed done on the ranch in the coming days. Despite Noah's help over the last couple of days, there were things that just didn't get done when the boss wasn't around, and they were behind. They weren't going to get any farther ahead with Ren stalking his thoughts, either. She was reluctant, she needed time—he had told her as much, and she hadn't argued. But he needed something more.

At the barn, he dismissed Finn and unsaddled the horses on his own, stewing in his own thoughts for far longer than was appropriate. The quiet chewing of the horses in their stalls should have soothed him but it just made space for more brooding.

When he finally made it into the house, he found Ren at the stove, working on dinner. He spotted Kerri and Gage in the living room reading together on his way to the bathroom to scrub up. He couldn't help but think how nice it was to come in at the end of the day to a warm, fragrant house filled with bodies he was happy to see.

After stopping to give Gage a hair ruffle and thank Kerri for taking the time to read to him, he emerged into the kitchen. He might have been imagining it but he noticed Ren stiffen a bit when he came into the room. She had been quiet and withdrawn at breakfast but he assumed it was the hangover. He leaned against the counter in much the same way he had when he had proposed they head to the dance hall. Oh how things had changed since that day. For him, anyways.

He'd known he wanted her from the first time he'd seen her, but after what transpired between them in the parking lot... well, it was like an addiction. He spent all day thinking about when he might get his next fix.

She carefully angled her face away from him as she worked away, keeping her eyes down. He frowned. She had been a welcoming, warm, soft relief last night, and now she almost cringed as he shifted, getting imperceptibly closer to her. He backed off a step, giving her some space.

~

Ren was relieved when Dane stepped back. A four foot radius was too close. She felt like she was barely hanging onto the threads of everything she had here—Kerri, this job, her sanity... and his proximity made it so much harder to remember why she was trying to keep control over all of those things in the first place.

"Are you okay?" He asked.

"Yes..."

"This is about last night, isn't it?"

She let out a long breath, paused from peeling her potatoes and looked up at him.

"We made a mistake. There's nothing to talk about, Dane," she said, wishing she were anywhere but there.

"That... that was no mistake, Ren." The intent in his voice made her insides tremble, thinking of the way his fingers had brushed over her flesh and elicited fire.

She couldn't respond.

He sighed, shifted again, closer to her. The part of her that normally made good judgment calls seemed to be malfunctioning with him so close. She knew she should look away, take a step back. Defiantly, she didn't break the eye contact.

"I don't make mistakes like that."

"We were drinking." She could feel her argument losing steam before she even said it.

"I knew what I was doing and did it because I wanted to. Did you?"

She realized the implications of her words. He inched closer, so close she could feel the heat radiating from his body, read the expression in his eyes that told her he was sincere.

"Yes."

"So we were both consenting adults."

"Yes."

"Then what's going on here, Ren?"

"I just don't think any good can come of this." She looked over her shoulder uneasily as she heard one of the kids turn on the television in the other room. "You're my boss."

"I know."

"So... we do this... whatever 'this' is. Something happens down the road and we have a fight and I'm out of a job—one of the only two good things I have going on in my life right now."

She swept her eyes over his body regretfully.

"And my life is complicated, Dane. You're better off if your only involvement is to sign my paychecks."

"If you want me to leave you alone, have nothing to do with you but signing your checks... just say the word. If that's what you *really* want, I won't bother you anymore." He reached across the minuscule space between them and cupped her jaw in his big hand, lifting her eyes to meet his. This time, she didn't move away, relishing his touch. She closed her eyes briefly and swallowed, knowing what would come next, welcoming it. Her belly quivered at his closeness and she let out a long, heated breath.

She'd recited the script she'd been rehearsing in her mind since she'd gotten up this morning, every word, and no matter how well rehearsed it was, he hadn't bought it. She wasn't sure *she* even believed it anymore.

"I don't want that." There. She'd said it. The words hung in the air between them only a moment before his mouth closed over hers, stopping any further discussion, and she went warm and soft in his arms, pushing closer to him as she surrendered. He turned her back to the counter, pinning her body lightly with his. Before she knew what she was doing, Ren snaked an arm around his neck, cupping the base of his neck, drawing him nearer, her free hand resting on his hip. Her body wanted his, it was a magnetism she had no control over.

For a moment, she forgot about her fears, the

kids in the next room, and all of her arguments about why this couldn't work. His closeness, the heat radiating from him - it was all-consuming. He slid his hand down her spine, lifting the hem of her shirt to rest his fingertips lightly against the bare skin of the small of her back and it was like a direct hit of adrenaline. Her mind fast-tracked back twenty-four hours to the tailgate of his truck and she let a soft sound into his mouth, pushing herself against him. Her brain might have told her what dangerous territory she was treading into but her body didn't care.

The feel of his lips against hers was addictive, and Ren didn't want to give up the drugs. As quickly as it started, it was over. Dane lifted his head, took a step back, and slid a hand down over her hair, pressing a gentle kiss to her forehead. That devastating half-smile tipped one corner of his lips as he took one last, long look at her, and then headed into the living room to gather up Kerri and Gage as if nothing had happened at all.

"Time to set the table, guys."

Ren watched his back for a moment, unmoving. The man did things to her insides she'd never felt before and right now, she was reeling. Sure, the brief flirtations and one-night stands of her life before Kerri had satisfied a physical need, but not only did Dane awaken the desire in her, he also triggered the mechanism that made her feel safe. She was wary of that mechanism, though—it had steered her into dangerous complacency before. She was determined not to go down that road again.

FOURTEEN

DANE KEPT HIS eyes trained on the little roan colt from Reicher as the horse circled him in the round pen. This time, he wore a saddle; his training had progressed considerably since that fateful day Gage had tumbled from the corral fence, and a few days later, Ren and Kerri had arrived in his life. Finally, he could focus all of his attention on the horse he had dubbed Diesel. The colt was built like a brick shithouse, broad body and short legs, but powerful.

Breathing a sigh of relief he didn't have to worry about where Gage was and what he was getting into, Dane sent the colt out in another circle around him. He knew his nephew was safe and happy, in the house or in the orchard with the girls, being nurtured in a way that really only a maternal figure could provide. It was the first time since he'd become his nephew's primary caretaker that he felt like he might have had an iota of control over his life, and was doing a half decent job of it... but he knew he couldn't have done any of it without Ren there. Hell, even Kerri did a great job keeping Gage occupied. While it certainly took away from the quantity of time Gage was hanging onto Dane and Finn's shirttails, he had to say it increased the quality of time he spent with his nephew. For once, he felt like he had his head above water when it came to being the child's guardian... and all it had taken was this woman.

Try as he might, he couldn't beg, bribe or bully her out of his mind. She occupied just about every spare second he wasn't thinking about something ranch related, and then she often found her way into those thoughts, too. When he thought about this latest string of horses they had in for training, he thought about how well matched Ren would look astride the leggy gray filly he had been working. When he was riding fence thinking about calving season, he thought of her sitting across the table at four am with a cup of hot coffee and a sleepy smile. In truth, there wasn't a single thought that was safe.

When he considered the long term, he saw Ren there. It was early to have these thoughts, but he understood now what Gavin meant when he'd told Dane 'when you know, you know' as the brothers had sat him down for a chat about his short engagement to June. They'd all thought him crazy and fanciful, and way too young to saddle himself to one woman for the rest of his life, but the youngest Baylor brother had displayed a clarity and assurance that Dane was beginning to understand, just a little.

Oh, she would need time. It was clear she didn't completely trust him or their life here at the ranch yet, but she would. He could help her, and failing that, he could be patient. Though he didn't know the extent of them yet, he knew she had demons dogging her, and he would fight those for her, too. There wasn't a single thing he wouldn't do for her.

Finally, Dane stopped pushing Diesel and the colt slowed to a walk, coming in to make a connection with him, just as he had been trained. He put his hand out and stroked the colt's nose lightly before moving to check the saddle and make sure it was secure. He hooked a rope to the horse's halter and turned his head toward him as he put a foot in the stirrup and bore a bit of weight on it. The colt looked at him, clearly processing this next step in the pair's journey together as in one smooth motion, Dane swung his leg over Diesel's back and settled himself in the saddle for the first time.

The colt relaxed with a long sigh and Dane stroked his neck reassuringly. Clucking, he urged him forward and he complied, breaking into a lazy trot around the round pen. This was the type of first ride Dane liked—a smart horse added together all of the training and had a sensible head when it came time for it. He'd sat on a few bronc blow outs but he preferred quiet and easy, just like this. Finn was game for a lot more explosive behavior, which was why he was so exceptional with troubled horses. At Dane's age, he didn't bounce quite so well anymore and anytime he could avoid getting hurt and not being able to work the ranch as effectively as he liked, he would.

He reined Diesel in the other direction and completed a couple of circles that way, smiling as the horse followed his guidance. A good brain like this one could be of use around the ranch. He gave the verbal cue for a stop as he noticed a feminine figure leaning against the rail of the round pen, watching him.

~

Ren had been observing for a couple of minutes, completely enthralled by the ease and patience with which Dane worked the horse. She remembered seeing him with the colt when she'd first arrived and she would never have guessed the horse would become quiet and relaxed as Dane so trustingly swung aboard.

While watching him with the horse calmed her spirit, her mind kept volleying over the events of the last couple of days. She couldn't figure out what it was he wanted out of all of this. Hell, she didn't know what *she* dared to want out of it. She had never allowed herself to want anything. Anita took everything from her, at one point or another.

Though the attraction between them was undeniable, she couldn't help but think about the what ifs... what if she made a home in Three Rivers, got comfortable, and then Dane changed his mind? She would have to start all over again. She'd have to find new work, uproot Kerri once again. And those were the devastating consequences if her mother *never* found them. Adding that potential threat made everything else that much worse.

She could want this, she knew. She probably already did if she let herself think about it for any amount of time. Wanting it was half of the battle. Dane wanted *her*, it could be as easy as saying yes, but it had been a long time since she'd put her heart on the line like this.

She watched him dismount, stroke the horse's neck lightly and then head toward her.

"How does he look?"

"He looks great... but I wouldn't know any different if he looked awful." Truth was, she hadn't paid much attention to the colt. It was the man who commanded all of her attention. This patient, giving, gentle man. He handled his young horses in much the same way he handled his nephew: providing him the opportunity to do the right thing and gently guiding him when he made the wrong decision.

Dane flashed her a smile that made her heart swell six sizes.

"Oh, you'll learn."

He moved toward the gate and she instinctively opened it.

"You missed dinner, but I kept you a plate. Kerri is reading to Gage, I think they're just about done in for the day." She fell into step beside him as they made their way toward the horse barn, Diesel moseying along beside Dane with his head down on the other side.

"Have I mentioned how much I appreciate you? If you weren't here, I'd still be trying to wrangle Gage inside for a microwave dinner, and then we'd fall asleep in front of the TV."

Ren smiled, shrugged. They walked in silence for a moment until their fingers brushed together and she startled a little, tucking her hands into her pockets.

"He likes the structure. I like the family."

"Me too."

Dane led Diesel into his stall, where the horse immediately buried his face in a pile of hay. Dane deftly undid the saddle fittings and slid it off of his back, exiting the stall to deposit it on a nearby rack.

"I don't know how you do it." Ren settled herself on a nearby bale of hay as Dane hung up a manure fork and checked each of the stalls for hay and clean water.

"Do what?" He slid in and out of a stall with a flake of hay for Roxy.

"These horses come in here wild as the wind. And then you turn them into soft little puppy dogs." She nodded toward Diesel, who had lifted his head to watch for a moment. The horse had been scared and maybe a little defiant from what Ren could tell when she had first arrived but now the colt's eyes tracked Dane's every move with interest and intelligence.

He settled on the bale of hay next to her, so close their arms brushed, and shrugged.

"You start easy... show them they have

nothing to be afraid of, that you're not gonna let them get hurt. Instead of forcing them into your way of thinking, you ask them to do stuff so that it's their idea. If they don't get it right the first time, you ask again. Until they answer it right. And then you end every session on a good note, so they can feel good about themselves. And you never do let 'em get hurt."

Ren swallowed heavily as Dane moved, reaching to cup her jaw. He brushed his thumb across her cheekbone. His eyes asked but her heart was racing too quickly for her to answer. He tipped her chin up and brought his mouth down over hers. She opened to him almost immediately, shifting closer in response.

The kiss was sweet, chaste. It tasted like promises and had none of the fervent desire in it Ren had experienced behind the dance hall or even in the kitchen. It was a dedication, a solemn vow that she could let go and he would catch her.

He broke away just a moment, his lips hovering not far from hers as his hand moved to stroke over her hair, their foreheads touching. "You know I'd never hurt you, right?"

She let out a shaky breath and nodded, closing the distance between their mouths eagerly to avoid having to give it too much more thought. She knew this kind, easygoing man wouldn't hurt her, but she couldn't say the same in the return. There could be a day when her mother would catch up to them and she'd have to leave him in a lurch; to protect herself, to protect Kerri. She could give herself up to him for now, but in the end, she was somebody who hurt other people. It wasn't intentional, it was self-preservation, but that rarely lessened the sting.

Before she'd taken Kerri, she'd dated; even lived with a boyfriend for a short period of time. Since then, there had been flirtations, one night stands, but no dating and no plans for the future. Beyond that, they just got attached, they had expectations. It was a lot harder to pack up all your things and sprint away in the night when someone was counting on you. Keeping her inner circle constricted to just herself and Kerri was the only way she'd figured out to keep from hurting others— in the process, she saved herself a lot of heartache, too.

The thought of damaging this man and his family, who had so generously opened their doors and their hearts to the Maddock girls made her chest tighten painfully. In the end, she could heal. She'd toughened up, scarred over emotional wounds to protect herself over and over in her lifetime. Did the sweet, soft hearts of the Baylors defend themselves that quickly? What if she was already in too deep?

Disrupting her thought process, Dane's stomach growled loudly and broke them apart with a chuckle.

"Suppose supper is in order." He slid his hand over her hair one more time. Ren could have gone on kissing him all night. Everything about him made her want to feel warm and safe, and she could suspend her reality, if only briefly, when he touched her.

She touched his cheek with a smile.

"You'll waste away to nothing if we don't feed you."

"Damn straight." He rose before she did and offered his hand to help her up. She took it without hesitation, and he didn't let go once she took hold. It made her smile despite her best effort not to.

Inside the house, Ren found Kerri sitting up in the living room, nose buried in her cell phone as it buzzed signifying text messages received. Ren had originally gotten the phone for Kerri so she could keep track of her. Any time she was out of sight, Ren felt anxious, and dropping a quick text had been an easy way to touch base and make sure everything was okay. Unfortunately, teenagers being teenagers, the phone got used for much more. Half the time, Ren felt that unless she was communicating via text, she was being ignored in favor of whoever was on the other end, sending Kerri messages.

Kerri looked up.

"Where's Dane?"

"Saying goodnight to Gage. Not long for you either, hey? We're touring the school tomorrow."

Kerri nodded, distracted as her phone made a buzzing noise, her eyes flitting to the screen. It vibrated a second time before she even had a chance to reply.

"Who's texting you so much anyways?"

"Nobody." The teenager shoved the phone

into her pocket.

"Hey, it's not that Sullivan kid, is it?" Ren's jaw tightened.

"I swear it's not. He's gross." Kerri clasped her hands together on her lap, the picture of innocence.

"I see. Well... not too late, okay?" Kerri was typically very open with Ren, and it bothered her that she wouldn't disclose the identity of her texter. Ren's general rule was not to pry too hard so as to keep the lines of communication open when they were necessary but the blatant secretiveness didn't sit well with her.

She told herself it was someone Kerri had met at the gymkhana night that Dane had taken her to. He'd assured her rodeo kids were good people—he had been one, after all, but she couldn't help but remember the scene in town with Kerri when they'd first arrived. She didn't know what she would have done without Dane there. Overall, Three Rivers was full of good people, but her thoughts wandered to Kyle Sullivan entirely too often. He reminded her that there was a whole slew of evil out there that she didn't already know.

Kerri grunted in response.

"Hey, eye contact." Irritated, Ren gestured between her eyes and her sister's with two fingers and the teen looked up, Ren's tone didn't welcome any questioning. "I mean it. Not too late."

The buzz of Kerri's phone told Ren this was a battle she hadn't won.

FIFTEEN

REN SIGHED AND shifted in bed, rolling over just as she heard Gage cry out from downstairs. She hadn't been about to sleep anyways—the encounter with Kerri and her cell phone was on her mind and so was Dane Baylor's sweet kiss in the barn.

She got up and headed for the door to the back staircase. It was the first time she'd had to use it in the time she'd been here, and she wondered if Dane would hear her coming down the stairs... if he had even heard Gage cry out.

She paused at the base of the stairs, noting that Dane's door was open just a crack. She knocked a couple of times on Gage's before pushing it open.

"Gage? Honey, are you okay?"

The boy was sobbing in his sheets. She moved through the room, mindful of toys on the floor, and perched beside him on the twin bed. "Close your eyes, I'm going to turn the light on."

Flicking on the bedside lamp, she turned back to Gage and brushed his sweat matted hair out of his eyes. Unexpectedly, he looked past her and recognition flickered in his eyes. His sobbing quieted.

"Uncle Dane, the monsters were here." She hadn't heard him come in but she looked over her shoulder to see Dane was standing in the doorway in nothing but a pair of boxer briefs. It was a bad time for desire to rush her, but she seemed not to have much control over that sort of thing these days. She sucked in a breath as he crossed the floor and settled on the other side of the bed. The boy immediately wrapped his arms around his uncle and Dane dropped his lips to the top of his strawberry blond head, giving him a strong hug. The tension dropped out of the boy's body almost immediately when his uncle hugged him and Ren could relate.

"Is it time for the spray?" Dane asked, pulling back a little bit. Gage nodded vigorously and Dane opened the bedside stand and pulled out a small aerosol can. "Where were they?"

Gage pointed toward his partially opened closet and Dane made an exaggerated show of spraying into it, then under the bed, and in the corner by the toy box for good measure at the boy's prompting.

Watching the little ritual was the first time Ren felt like a clear outsider to this family, but she didn't mind. While Dane had expressed reasonable doubt in his ability to parent his nephew, this was yet another piece of evidence that he was doing a better job than he thought he was.

Finally, Gage turned to her.

"Uncle Dane is the best monster fighter."

"Is he? He *is* pretty handy with that spray."

"It's monster spray. They are 'llergic to it and it makes them sneeze. If they can't stop sneezing, the monsters can't get me!"

Ren smiled, meeting Dane's eyes across the bed. Could this man fight the monster that was her mother if that was what it came down to? Maybe she could rebuild a life in Three Rivers if things went South between them, but there was no way she could stay if Anita found them.

"It sounds like your Uncle Dane has got these monsters under control."

Gage nodded, squeezing his teddy bear to his chest and nestled down into the bed.

"Alright, buddy. You go back to sleep now. You know I'm just across the hall."

The boy nodded again as Dane pulled the blankets up to his chin and kissed his forehead.

"Good night again," Dane said.

"Good night again." Gage repeated back to him without hesitation.

Dane nodded to Ren across the bed and she ruffled Gage's hair lightly, then pressed her lips to the same spot Dane had and rose. As they filed out of the bedroom, he pulled the door shut carefully behind them.

There was something about him, so vulnerable, sleep rumpled in just his boxer briefs.

Mouth dry, she tried to be covert as her eyes slid over the body she had only ever seen hints of. The tanned ridges of muscles in his arms and torso attested to hours spent working in the hay fields. Sculpted abs tapered down to a narrow waist, a tantalizing trail of hair leading her eyes lower than was appropriate. She stopped herself, cleared her throat, and painstakingly dragged her eyes up to meet his. He had that same expression on his face that she remembered from the dance floor, two beats before he'd kissed her.

She didn't give him the opportunity to make the first move this time and crossed the distance between them in the landing with certainty. She was giving him her clear, unequivocal answer. Yes, they would pursue this and deal with the consequences later. Yes, she would give herself to him and the four of them would be a family. She slid her hand over his shoulder, to the back of his neck and levied herself up on her toes to meet his mouth.

Ren didn't have the upper hand for long. Dane met the kiss aggressively, his hand moving over her hip, under the edge of her t-shirt, to the bare, soft skin of her lower back and tugged her tight to him. This time, there were no thick layers of denim and cotton separating them and she felt his warm skin and hard body through the flimsy shirt she wore. Her flesh raised in anticipation as his fingertips slid across it. The heat of what had transpired behind the dance hall paled in comparison to the inferno he ignited in her now.

She eased backwards, toward his bedroom door, meaning to finish what they'd started two nights ago—this time, without an ounce of regret or angst.

~

Dane still wasn't sure it hadn't been a dream to find Ren in Gage's room comforting him with little more than a t-shirt and a pair of boy-cut panties on—but this was a real flesh and blood woman under his hands—the very same woman he had been dreaming of since she'd marched into his home and his heart. Here she was, willing, wanting. She sure as hell didn't have to ask twice.

Pushing through the door of the bedroom, he kicked it shut behind them, barely breaking the kiss. Her hand fisted in his hair lightly and he bit back a groan. He backed her all the way up until the back of her knees hit the edge of his bed and she sank down onto it.

Ren leaned back on her hands, tipping her head with a little smile that made him hard as hell. He dropped to his knees beside the bed, sliding his hands under her shirt over her sides, drawing the fabric up with him as he went. His lips landed near her navel and she squirmed a little. Eventually, his lips moved North with his hands, pushing her back onto the bed, bit by bit, his body hovering over hers until he found her lips again, claiming them with a fiery kiss. It lasted only an instant until he pulled her shirt over her head, and took in the sight of her in all of her glory.

"This evens the playing field a little, doesn't it?" Her voice was teasingly innocent. He chuckled against the hot skin of her throat, skimming his fingertips over her nipples, just enough to tease them to attention, making her arch up into his hand.

"You could say that." He pulled his head back and caught her eyes, remembering her earlier regret. "I need to know this is what you want, Ren."

There was not an ounce of resistance in this woman now, as he tracked his fingers over her soft flesh, but he knew he couldn't live with himself if she had even a second of doubt about what was happening right now. He would go as slow as it took, worship her in the way she deserved, and give her all of the pleasure she could handle, but he needed to have her permission to do so.

She nearly undid him when she let out a heated breath and reached for him, drawing his lips to hers until they were barely brushing against each other. "Yes."

~

Ren arched her body upward as Dane claimed her mouth once more. She couldn't get close enough. She was coiled tight as a spring, in anticipation of what she knew his masterful hand and gentle touch could produce. Though she'd resisted at first, she'd thought of this moment time and time again. Her fingers splayed over the smooth muscles of his shoulder as he bent his head, drawing the sensitive flesh of her throat into his mouth to suckle and nip lightly. A shot of pleasure coursed through her veins and she let a soft noise as his teeth and tongue worked over her sensitive flesh.

He moved lower, now, his mouth finding her nipple and treating it the same as her throat. She stifled a whimper with her teeth vised tightly on her lower lip; his hand moved lower, lower, found the waistband of the panties and slid his fingers inside. Pausing just a moment before he touched the most intimate part of her, he lifted his head and made eye contact with her.

"Okay?"

She nodded, breathless and he forged ahead, taking the same painfully slow trek across her sensitive center. It was almost playful, the leisurely way he strummed the chords of her body, but Ren came quickly this time, breathless, calling his name. She couldn't think of a single thing that felt better than his touch on her skin. A wrenching groan rumbled deep in his chest as she whimpered and writhed against him, desperate for more.

There wasn't an ounce of hesitation between them as he moved down her body, drawing her panties over her thighs and following their trail with his lips. He held her gaze without breaking, the spark of passion telling her every move was deliberate, reverent, and sincere. Her skin tingled under the touch of his lips and fingertips. He moved back up her body, sliding his hands over the curve of her hips and then cupping her breasts with his palms. He tweaked each nipple in turn, a mischievous smirk playing over his features as she first winced, then pushed into the sensation.

Shifting, Dane positioned himself between her knees and Ren tensed with anticipation. Every second he had stood too close, looked too long, and she did the same, culminated as he entered her slowly, inch by inch until he was seated deep and she thought she would come undone without any effort at all. A shuddering groan moved through his body. He waited just a moment to allow her body to accommodate him and then began to withdraw.

Ren dug her fingers into his shoulders as he eased back, desperate not to end their contact. He slid one big hand along her thigh to hitch her knee up around his hip and surged into her as the other drew one of her hands above her head to clasp against the mattress, increasing the amount of skin on skin contact and bringing him even closer.

As with everything he did, Dane's rhythm was consistent, patient and compelling. Ren's second orgasm built slowly this time, steady, starting deep at the ends of her toes and working its way up, burning her up from the inside out. He peppered kisses along her throat and collarbone, catching her mouth occasionally as she crested toward her peak.

"Dane!" She whimpered, clamping her lip firmly between her teeth to avoid the sort of volume that would alert the kids to what was going on, her fingers pressing deep into the flesh at his hip.

"Just let go, Ren." That lazy smile crossed his

lips but she could tell he was teetering close to the edge, his eyes dark and his brow furrowed lightly.

Suddenly, Ren was shattering, shuddering as Dane's movements picked up speed, driving her relentlessly, their voices rising together as she watched her normally unflappable cowboy lose control with her.

~

Dane couldn't imagine anything better than lying in his bed, Ren curled up with her head on his bicep, her naked body pressed to the length of his. It occurred to him that maybe he'd never actually made love to a woman until now. The warm afterglow was like nothing else he'd ever experienced before. He pulled her toward him, pressing a gentle kiss to her forehead as she stretched her body, catlike. His eyes were heavy and his breathing slow; it had been another long day at the ranch and he was tuckered but he wouldn't have missed out on this for the world.

She started to pull away from him and he let out a complainant moan, rolling her back toward him with his arm around her shoulders.

"Stay."

She pressed a kiss to his cheek and laughed a little.

"One, I'm not a dog. Two, I can't stay. What if Kerri needs me in the night? She'll panic if I'm not there."

With his eyes closed, he grumbled again but

released her.

"Fine. But you should know the only reason I'm letting you go is because I'm too tired to fight you. Find yourself here again and you might not be so lucky next time."

He felt her sit up on the bed, leaning over him on her knees. Her breasts brushed against his chest as she crossed his body to drag her teeth playfully over his lower lip, bringing around a familiar tightening in his groin.

"*If* there's a next time." He could hear the wicked smile on her voice.

Without warning and without opening his eyes, he tugged her sideways to straddle his waist. The softest noise slipped through her lips but he could tell she was as turned on by the skin to skin contact as he was.

"Oh there'll be a next time." He smirked and opened his eyes. The light and playfulness in hers was promising. He tugged her down for a quick kiss and then helped push her off of him, giving her bottom a playful swat. "Fine. Go back to your bed. I'll just be down here all lonely."

She got to her feet and rounded the end of the bed, tapping his toe lightly as she passed by. "It's better this way and we both know it."

He watched her go, his hands tucked behind his head. She closed the door most of the way behind her and he listened for her footsteps on the stairs, smiling to himself as he let his eyes slide shut again.

He would do anything to keep this woman in

his home, in his heart. He could still feel the warmth of her skin on his and he couldn't think of any other way he wanted to exist.

SIXTEEN

"LUCKY!" GAGE SQUEALED with delight and leapt from the passenger seat of Dane's pick-up truck almost before he had it in park.

"Hey! Be careful." But he couldn't help laughing as the child bowled into the fluffiest golden retriever puppy he had ever seen on his mother's front lawn. He was halfway convinced Lucky thought Gage was another puppy, hell, *he* was halfway convinced Gage was a puppy most of the time. Little boys were not all that different from little dogs, he had surmised. Dane got out of the truck and let the door fall shut behind him.

Ren and Kerri had gone into town to shop and catch a movie—some much needed quiet time, and much as he hated to admit it, he was jealous that it wasn't him taking her out on the town and spending time with her. For now, she preferred to keep everything under wraps. She said it was for the sake of his family, but he definitely felt there was something deeper at work behind those pretty hazel eyes that had more to do with her own family than his.

"Hey mama." Giving his mother a brief hug and a kiss on the cheek, he observed Gage playing chase with the puppy for a moment before he whistled, catching the boy's attention. He tipped his head in Ella's direction, indicating that Gage should give her the same kind of greeting.

"Nana invited you for supper, least you can do is say hello to her. Lucky will still be there."

The boy remembered himself and ran full tilt for Ella, skidding to a stop just inches before he threw his arms around her legs and gave her a joyous squeeze. If nothing, he had not lost even an ounce of his loving nature despite losing his parents, and it was moments like these that made Dane proud of the job he had done raising him for the last couple of years.

Ella ruffled his strawberry blond hair and hugged him back before sending him off again. "I filled up the play pool for you and Lucky to splash in."

Gage's eyes lit up as he and the puppy took off at breakneck speed for the small plastic pool at the corner of the yard, leaving Dane alone with his mother.

"I made you a coffee." She gestured to the porch where a couple of steaming mugs sat between the porch swing and a rocking chair—both of them providing ample access to watch the boy and the puppy playing.

Dane took the steps a couple at a time and lowered himself onto the swing. The rocker had always been his mama's spot and always would be. She sank into it easily and took up her mug without looking at him.

"Finn tells me you've been spending a lot of time with the Maddock girl."

He couldn't tell a thing from her tone, and he quirked a brow, casting a suspicious look in her direction.

"Well, she *is* living at the ranch, helping me with Gage. Ain't really easy to *not* spend time with her." He realized belatedly that in a small town like Three Rivers, gossip about the little display they had put on at the dance hall a few weeks before would have likely gotten around to his mama already—this just happened to be the first chance she had to talk to him about it.

The pointed look Ella gave her son told him she was looking for more explanation. It was a look Dane knew all too well from growing up—the one that coaxed the guiltiest confessions out of the boys. He could feel a flush creeping up his neck. His mama knew exactly what was going on—she always did—and he wouldn't be able to hide a thing from her. He could try, though.

"There's nothing going on."

"Don't tell me there's nothing going on when there is *clearly* something going on, Dane. I've known you longer than you've known yourself, I can *tell* when you're not telling your mama the truth."

He shifted uncomfortably, steeling himself with a long drag from his coffee cup.

"She seems like a nice girl, honey. Fits right in with the family, and Gage clearly loves her." Ella continued, in an obvious attempt to coax the real truth out of her eldest son.

Maybe this wouldn't be as painful as he had anticipated. He nodded slowly as his mother listed Ren's good points—she was really just scratching the surface. There was so much more. She was kind, thoughtful, adventurous; she was pretty as a picture and she made his blood sing when they touched. She'd taken to riding like a fish to water, had no fear of any of the livestock, and Rex loved her twice as much as Gage did. Kerri had developed a great rapport with both Dane and Finn and took great pleasure in assisting with the chores as often as she could. He couldn't remember what it felt like to live in the big house at the ranch *without* the Maddock girls underfoot, and he wasn't sure he wanted to.

"Does it look bad, though? Like I'm taking advantage of her, or I mail ordered a woman?" Truthfully, Dane didn't care what other people thought, but his mama... that was a whole 'nother story, right there.

Ella paused thoughtfully.

"Do *you* feel like you're taking advantage of her or that you mail ordered a bride?"

Bride... that was a word he hadn't considered.

"I feel like I might be falling in love with her."

His mother's knowing smile said it all. She looked like the cat that ate the canary and Dane would never hear the end of it. Someday, decades from now, she would draw it up out of memory and *still* be crowing about how she had been aware of what was going on even before Dane himself knew.

"Why do I get the feeling like you planned this all along, mama?"

Ella chuckled. "Well, *I* didn't plan it, but a power stronger than you certainly did."

Dane resisted the urge to roll his eyes at his mother and leaned back onto the swing with his coffee cup in hand, his long legs stretched out before him.

"So what do I do now?"

"You know, Dane, you've always been a smart boy. I never imagined I'd have to spell it out for you what you ought to do with a woman." Ella's tone was teasing.

Dane looked at her expectantly. While he was independent, he never had a problem deferring to his mother—she did, after all, have a few years on him, and a bit more life mileage to boot. Particularly when it came to women, she had the upper hand. He hadn't always lived by that philosophy but he got hurt a hell of a lot less now that he did.

"You *love* her, you fool." Ella insisted when Dane didn't reply. She chuckled to herself, shook her head, and rose to call for Gage and Lucky.

Dane let himself roll his eyes this time, shaking his head at his mother, and rising with his empty coffee mug in hand.

"Hey, I know you wanna gloat, but maybe

keep it under wraps for a bit before you start planning the wedding? I've only just convinced her that this is okay," he teased, referencing his mother's earlier inference about a mail order bride. Ella loved her family fiercely, including any additions by marriage, and had been over the moon when Gavin and June had announced their pregnancy with Gage. Though she had always recognized Dane had a lot on his plate between the ranch and caring for Gage, he was not completely immune to her occasional comment urging him to give a nice girl in town a second thought or even a second spin around the dance floor.

"I'll give you a couple weeks head start, how does that sound?" Ella was still laughing when she ushered Gage and Lucky into the house.

SEVENTEEN

"THIS ONE?" KERRI held a top up in front of her that Ren could tell without her even trying it on would show entirely too much of her sister's cleavage. Ren was barely ready to accept its presence in the first place, never mind it being in the line of vision of teen aged boys or even within a hundred miles of Kyle Sullivan.

"Not a chance, lady." Ren handed her one with a more modest neckline. If they could wrangle her into jeans that weren't painted on either, she'd be a happy woman. What was it with kids and the clothes they barely wore these days? She'd never been able to afford to deck Kerri out in all of the latest fashions, but somehow, a piece or two of trendy and barely-there clothing always found itself into her sister's wardrobe.

"So, I think Dane likes you." Kerri spoke loudly from the dressing room where she had disappeared with the shirt. Ren checked the area frantically and was relieved to find the back of the store empty. Evidenced by their time at the dance hall, everybody knew everybody in this town and she wasn't quite ready for her budding relationship with Dane to hit newsstands.

"Hey, shut up!" she hissed.

"Ooh, so *you* like *Dane!*" Kerri nearly crowed with laughter.

Ren rushed the door, poking her head inside and giving her sister, who was midway through changing shirts the dirtiest look she could.

"Quit, seriously. I want to keep my job. *You* want me to keep my job, so I can buy you that top. Which looks really good, by the way."

Kerri poked her tongue out, then examined herself in the mirror, deciding to add the shirt to the pile of clothing she had selected as acceptable. The girl's eyes held a spark of playfulness Ren hadn't genuinely seen in some time. It was the first time in a long time they weren't pinching pennies to pay rent and groceries and could actually do a little bit of shopping without adding every cent on every price tag together to make sure they didn't come up short at the till. They said money couldn't buy happiness, but Ren had decided when you were dealing with a fifteen year old, it sure didn't hurt.

They made their way to the front of the shop with their arms filled with clothes and deposited them on the counter in front of a bored looking girl around Ren's age. She was a tall bottle blond with a plain face and tight clothes. She lit up when she saw them.

"Hey, you're Dane Baylor's new housekeeper, right?"

"Sort of, yeah." Ren nodded, passing the articles of clothing to the girl.

"He's a dish, isn't he?"

Ren smiled but shrugged noncommittally. "He's a good *boss*." On the last word, Ren shot her sister a pointed look.

"I went out with him once. It never went anywhere, but we're both a little older now." The cashier, whose name tag read 'Sondra' chatted, her tone conversational and far too familiar as she rang each of their items through. "You know, maybe you could drop a good word for me? It'd be helpful, having 'someone on the inside', you know?"

"I'll do that." She offered the girl a kind smile and grabbed Kerri, who had been standing nearby open-mouthed at the cashier's brazenness, by the arm, pulling her out of the store. "Have a nice day!"

"What the...?" Kerri's voice was shrill and all too loud.

"Shut *up*." Ren didn't let go of her sister's arm as she dragged her across the parking lot.

Once they were inside the sedan Dane had insisted they take, Kerri narrowed Ren in her sights.

"Did she just think you would invite the guy *you* like on a date for her?" Her tone incredulous, Kerri's eyes were wide. "Do girls just *do* that?"

"Again, he is my *boss*, but yes, girls do that. Some girls think everything they see belongs to them." Ren turned the key in the ignition. "Seat belt."

Kerri slipped the belt over her shoulder. "You did it again, you know."

"Did what?"

"That thing where you don't answer my question so you don't have to lie to me."

Ren rolled her eyes.

"Ren Katherine Maddock. Do not roll your eyes at me." Kerri mimicked Ren's sternest tone with amazing accuracy.

Ren stuck her tongue out at her sister, guiding the car out of the shop's parking lot. She considered Sondra and her request... maybe she wasn't ready to make headlines but now that she'd made up her mind, she wasn't giving up Dane Baylor for anybody.

EIGHTEEN

REN STRAIGHTENED UP and arched her back, stretching out the cramp she'd gotten from bending over the weeds in the garden for the last thirty minutes. She had never been in one place long enough to have a garden so she wasn't one hundred percent sure what she was doing but she found the work soothing and it gave her something to do, particularly on these quiet Friday nights.

She'd met plenty of people in town but had yet to make any acquaintances she could really consider 'friends'. It might have been her inclination not to put down roots or it could have come from her desire to safeguard the burgeoning relationship with Dane, but she hadn't found anyone compelling enough to open up to.

"Mama would be some proud of this." Dane's voice startled her, she hadn't heard him approach and who knew how long he had been standing there watching her digging in the dirt like a kid.

"You think?" She smiled up at him from her kneeling position and wiped at her face. Ella Baylor had very quickly become the most trustworthy woman she knew. She always had additional insight on Gage when it was needed and Ren had even asked her for help with Kerri on the occasional phone call.

He nodded solemnly.

"Know what else I think?" He crouched down next to her, leaning close enough to brush a bit of dirt off of her cheek with his thumb. He didn't take his hand away when he was done, but cupped her jaw and tilted her gaze up to meet his. Her heart skipped two beats before she had the sense to think about anything but the desire in his eyes. "I think it's sexy as hell when you play pioneer woman out here."

Ren glanced quickly behind him, checking for children in earshot but they had been tasked to clean up after dinner and she hadn't seen a sign of them yet. One corner of her lips tipped up. She'd never felt so desired, so beautiful, as when Dane Baylor set his eyes on her the way he had right now. It was as pleasurable as a physical touch.

"When are you going to let me take you out and show you off to the world, Ren?" His voice was low and rough.

"You take me out all the time." She was being coy, attempting to lighten the mood. They went out in public with the kids in tow often, usually running errands. To the stander-by, it was as platonic as they came, a straight employer-employee relationship. In truth, there were long looks, brushing hands, simple touches; things nobody else would have ever caught but that meant the world to her.

A frown furrowed his brow. "You know what I mean."

She was still reluctant. In their own little world, in the privacy of his bedroom, she could forget about the implications of their relationship, forget the scars Anita had laid on her emotionally and physically, and the fear that she would not be able to finish what she started. She had become all too aware that the Baylors were a prominent and well respected family in town, particularly the three brothers. It seemed they could do no wrong—women wanted to be with them, men wanted to *be* them. People would notice where Dane laid his affections, and after she had gone, they would ask, flaying open any carefully mended wounds with good intentions the same way Mrs. Bates had in the grocery store.

She offered him a playful smile.

"I know where you can take me out tonight." The hopeful look in his eyes made her heart seize. "Fair's in town, isn't it? Bet the kids would love to go."

His handsome smile melted her just a little and lightened the mood entirely. It wasn't exactly what he'd meant and she knew it, but she was throwing him a little bone. It was the best she could let herself do right now, and he showed his appreciation.

"Gage *has* been asking to go. They're barrel racing tonight and he loves to watch."

"Good, then, we'll go to the fair tonight." She tipped back on her heels, dusted her hands off and they rose together, heading toward the house to gather up the kids.

It took Ren less than fifteen minutes to convince the extremely enthused Kerri and Gage to finish the post-dinner chores they had been dawdling over, wash faces and hands, and head for Dane's truck.

The fairgrounds weren't far from the Baylor's store and it took them less than ten minutes to get there. The parking lot was filled to overflowing; like the dance hall had been the night she had gone with Dane. That seemed so many days and emotions ago. Her heart was lighter now—still cautious, but less burdened.

In the distance, she could see the ferris wheel rising high against the dusky skyline and Gage shouted, excited at the sight of it. Dane parked the truck in one of the only available spots and the kids poured out ahead of them.

"Hey! Not too far ahead! And hold hands!" Ren shouted after them, and they paused long enough to lock their fingers together as they raced toward the bright lights of the midway. Dane took her command to heart and promptly slid her hand into his, twining their fingers together as they walked through the dark parking lot. She allowed it, a thrill lifting through her belly, but loosened her grip once they approached the admission booth where Kerri and Gage were waiting for them, looking through the gate and excitedly discussing which rides and attractions they wanted to see first.

Dane laughed at their excitement and approached the box, pulling his wallet out of his back pocket.

"How many? Oh hey, Dane." Ren would have recognized the bottle blonde's voice a mile away. Sondra, from the clothing shop. Resisting the urge to make a face at the woman, Ren hung back to keep an eye on the kids while Sondra leaned forward on her elbows, offering Dane an ample view of her cleavage as she twisted her long ponytail around one finger. "One adult, one child?"

Her eyes slid past him and landed on Ren, her cheery smile still fixed in place, and she waved. When Dane turned his head to glance at Ren, Sondra raised her eyebrow and jerked her chin in Dane's direction with a questioning look. Ren just shrugged.

"Actually, two adults, two children." Dane said, ushering Ren forward. She stepped forward, but didn't take his offered hand. "The *family* pass."

As she realized the implication of Dane's words, Sondra's expression soured, as if she'd smelled something off.

"I see. Well, you guys have fun!" She handed him the admission bracelets.

"We will." Ren couldn't resist giving the other girl a slightly smug smile as the four of them marched through the gates onto the midway. Of course, it was petty of her, but she couldn't think of a time in her life when she had something another person had wanted; between her dead father, her awful mother, the responsibility of her sister way before she was ready; there was little someone else could envy... until Dane Baylor.

Gage's eyes were as big as saucers as he took in all of the sights. Ren was sure he had been to a county fair before, considering how well-attended this one was, but it might have been the first year he really cared enough to be excited.

"I wanna go on the teacups! And the ferris wheel! And I wanna eat cotton candy!" Kerri still held one of his hands but Ren dropped her hand on his shoulder lightly, then ruffled his hair.

"Easy bud, we'll get everything. And there's barrel racing, too, remember?" Dane reminded him.

The boy's eyes lit up at the mention of his favorite sport and Ren could tell he was resisting the urge to surge ahead to find the barns.

"*I* do barrel racing with Chessy." Gage informed the girls, his chest puffing proudly. "But uncle Dane said I can't go again until my cast is off." He made a scowling face at the bright green fiberglass cast on his arm.

"Just another week now," Ren reminded him. They had circled the doctor's appointment on the calendar a few nights before when Gage had been particularly frustrated that he couldn't ride his bike.

Ren started when she felt Dane's palm find the small of her back, tightening their group up as they navigated through a busy part of the midway heading toward the arena. Once they cleared the crowd, he didn't move it. At his defiant action, she skeptically arched a brow at him. He shrugged innocently and continued to guide their group across the fairgrounds.

The huge arena where the races were being held was lit by several floodlights and a crowd of people and horses milled around while loud, bass-thumping music played. The grandstands were packed but somehow, Gage managed to pick Ella and Caine out of the crew and dropped Kerri's hand to wave frantically and run ahead of them.

Ren halfway expected Dane's hand to move away from her back when he saw his parents, but it didn't happen - instead he slid it down, patting her bottom affectionately as she started up the stairs ahead of him. A deep flush crept up her neck, a blend of embarrassment and pleasure. Even when her father had been alive and life hadn't been all that difficult, the *right* kind of boy had never paid her any attention and it felt good to have that now.

Ella had wedged herself in tight to Caine to make space on the bench seats beside them but there was still barely enough space for Kerri, Ren and Dane, even with Gage on Ella's lap. Climbing the bleachers ahead of them, Kerri slid in next to Ella and shrugged innocently as she gestured to the tiny space next to her.

Dane was close behind her, speaking in her ear. "You could..."

"I'm *not* sitting on your lap." She practically hissed at him, but she could tell from the smirking grin on Kerri's face that she'd heard every damn word.

Shooting daggers at Dane, she slid in so close to her sister, their hips touched. Kerri couldn't stop giggling, and it was infectious. She should have known there was no sense in hiding what was going on between her and Dane from Kerri. Gage wasn't perceptive enough to figure it out but Kerri had a lot of time on her hands to observe and draw her own conclusions, despite Ren's protests.

Taking what was the equivalent of half of a seat, Dane happily jammed in beside Ren on the end of the bench. With the width of his shoulders posing a problem, he slid his arm in behind her and with absolutely no hesitation, his fingers into the back pocket of her jeans. When she shot him a look, he shrugged.

"More space this way."

Ren held him in her unimpressed gaze for a moment longer and then turned her attention to the arena where they'd turned the music down and were preparing to announce the racers. The first few were a mix of male and female riders, and when Kerri asked, having only seen female barrel racers on TV, Dane explained that it seemed to only be that way at the top levels, and that the adrenaline rush of a fifteen second run knew no gender roles. He gave them a play-by-play as one rider after another came through, attempting to execute the turns around the barrels with the most efficiency and speed. The jubilant mood in the stands was infectious and it wasn't long before Ren and Kerri were whooping along with everyone else while riders urged their horses down the straightaway at top speeds to 'bring them home' and stop the timer.

The loudspeaker crackled. "In the ring now, our last rider - number sixteen, Noah Baylor and Blackjack."

Surprised, Ren found herself rushed to her feet as the crowd cheered. Clearly, the pair were a favorite. Noah entered the ring, circling his horse as the announcer advised him to start whenever he was ready. He turned his horse to face the grandstand and tipped his cowboy hat, drawing an unequivocally feminine squeal from the crowd before setting Blackjack onto the pattern. It was a thing of beauty, the way his horse ate up the ground between barrels, circling tight and clean around each one.

There wasn't a single behind still sitting in its seat when he turned Blackjack for the finish line. They all watched and cheered as his time flashed on a large digital screen across the arena and his name appeared at the top of the list of competitors. Gage was nearly vibrating with excitement. "Woo woo! Uncle Noah!" He pumped his fist and jumped up and down with enthusiasm until Caine swept him up and shucked him over his shoulder like Ren had seen Dane do with a bag of feed a hundred times already.

Suddenly, the stands were emptying and they were being swept down the stairs.

"Time for cotton candy!" Caine growled playfully. The boy squealed and Dane shot his father a look.

"You're not sending him home full of sugar and bouncing off the walls for Ren and I are you?"

The Baylor patriarch put on his best innocent expression and shook his head in response.

"The first grand kid is the one we make all the mistakes with. Make some more so we can do it the right way." Caine nudged Dane, giving him a conspiratorial wink.

At the bottom of the steps, the group made their way through the crowd to congratulate Noah on his win, then decided to split ways, on Ella's insistence that she wanted to go on a couple of rides with Gage and Kerri. It warmed Ren's heart, the way Caine and Ella had accepted Kerri as if she were their own kin. She attempted to give Kerri some cash for ride tickets and food but Ella waved them off.

"You kids go have fun. Everybody gets a night off." Ella gave Dane a smile that was just a little too knowing as far as Ren was concerned, and with that, they were off.

NINETEEN

DANE RESISTED THE urge to tuck Ren under his arm protectively as they left the grandstands and the rest of the family behind. He knew his mother was up to something when she'd commandeered the kids and sent him away with Ren, but he wasn't sure precisely what was going on in her head. His mother had always had an uncanny way of sussing out what the heart desired and altering the fates to play in the best favor of everyone involved. Judging by her enthusiasm when he'd been by her place for dinner last week, he guessed she was dipping her fingers into this one.

He couldn't say he was irritated about it. Whether Ren realized it or not, she belonged with him, with the Baylor family, and if his mother had a hand in helping that to happen, he was grateful for the assistance. It was obvious Ren appreciated and was damn good at her job, but he was beginning to feel like she was poised with one foot out the door.

He could hardly blame her, considering everything she'd told him, but he wanted her to feel like she was a part of the family, that she belonged with him and that he would do whatever he had to do to defend her from the demons of her past.

He guided her back out toward the midway. As often happened when they were in public, he ran into many familiar faces but he kept their conversations brief, focusing his attention on Ren. She took in the games, the vendors, and the rides as if she hadn't seen them in a very long time, if at all. At times, she was so engrossed in the lights and glitz he had to navigate them around foot traffic to avoid a collision.

After a time, she spoke. "I honestly haven't been to the fair since before my dad passed." The melancholy smile that tipped the corners of her lips told him she was walking back through memories she had long ago buried. "He used to love to bring me. Kerri was just little, about Gage's age, probably, the last time she was at a fair."

"He sounds like he was a good man."

"He was. I miss him all the time. He was definitely my best friend. I felt all alone for a long time after he died."

It was against his better judgment but he took her up into his arms, pressed a chaste kiss to her forehead. He knew she might mind, but he didn't care if a picture of it was splashed all over the front page of the *Three Rivers Chronicle*. When a woman, especially one he felt so strongly about, needed comfort, he wasn't going to stand by like an asshole.

She didn't resist like he expected her to but relaxed into his arms for a moment. It felt right.

"Do you wanna play a game?" She tipped her head back to catch his eyes, seeming to have gained the strength and comfort he'd hoped to pass on with his touch.

A slow smile drew across his lips. "Which one?"

She pointed at a nearby booth where he could see balloons pinned to a wall behind the man operating the game. The goal was to burst the balloon covering the odd colored star for the biggest prize—a combination of sharp shooting and luck.

"Dad never let me do the shooting ones. So let's make some new fair memories."

Dane knew that the time he would say no to Ren was rare, and the sparkle in her eye when she pointed out the game told him this was not even going to come close to the list.

"Alright."

They headed toward the booth and Dane laid down the money for each of them to pick up an air rifle. He watched Ren as she gripped hers. "You know what you're doing?"

She shrugged, held it up and peeked through the sight. "Point, pull the trigger, pop the balloon, kick your ass." She flashed a smile at him that warmed his heart.

"*If* I let you win."

He watched her analyzing the process, lifting the gun to her shoulder and pretending to pull the trigger a couple of times. It was cute as hell and it didn't take her long to figure it out; further evidence to the independent woman she was. They stood side by side, aiming at a target for practice shots Dane didn't really need. He was proficient with a rifle and usually bagged a deer every year to add some variety to the freezer. He'd grown up with a gun in his hands and had been using one to run off threats to the livestock as long as he could remember. Ren hit half of her targets and swore she wasn't trying to hit the ones she missed.

~

"Need a lesson, angel?" Ren stiffened as a pair of unfamiliar hands slid along her arms and she felt a body settle behind her. She dropped her air rifle and tried to jerk away but he had her enveloped firmly in his grip.

"Damnit, what is it about you Sullivan boys and your lack of respect?" Dane's gun clattered to the counter and he grabbed hold of the man's collar. Just a hair shorter than Dane and lacking his muscle, the other man held up his hands as if he were innocent but Dane was already pushing him backwards into the side of the booth. "You don't lay your hands on a woman unless she asks for it."

Ren jumped free of the altercation and got a look at the man who had accosted her. He looked like the grown up version of the teen who had been asking about Kerri's breasts and she could only guess this might be the older brother. He was struggling while Dane held him pinned against the wall. It was different to see him behave in a way that was anything but patient and gentle but she couldn't say she didn't appreciate that he stepped in. She rubbed her hands down over her arms as if to get the feel of the other man off.

"Hey look, she just looked like she needed help. And she hasn't got a sign on her saying she belongs to anybody."

Dane drew back a fist like he was going to hit the man but then dropped it, lifted him away from the wall and then shoved him back against it before releasing him.

"She belongs to herself, and if she didn't ask for any help, she didn't need it." He turned to stalk off, presumably before he made good on his threat to hit the man. Ren looked over her shoulder as Dane ushered her away and the Sullivan man's face was ashen.

"You know if you don't put a mark on her, somebody else will snatch that tasty morsel right out from under your nose, Baylor," he called after them.

Ren felt sick to her stomach to be boiled down to little more than a piece of meat, as if she weren't even there. She shivered and moved to Dane's side, sliding her arm around his waist. Maybe she didn't want to go public with all of this yet but she wanted to send a clear message to the man who had touched her against her will. Dane closed his arm around her shoulders, drawing her in tightly and pressed a kiss to her temple before they began to move through the fairgrounds, neither of them giving the man a second look.

Casting a mischievous glance her way, Dane pulled them into the line at the ferris wheel. Quickly the cars filled with couples and small groups. When it came their turn, Ren didn't give it a second thought as he took her hand and they crossed the gang plank to get onto the ride. She snuggled in next to him, eager to rid her mind of the feel of the stranger's hands on her. The wheel lifted them higher in the air, bit by bit, as the remaining cars were filled.

The fairgrounds spread out below them, loud and smelling of diesel and popcorn. The colored lights of the different rides looked like twinkling jewels—it was beautiful and brought a rush of memories back to Ren. Dane slid an arm over her shoulders and she melted into his side easily, letting out a soft sigh. They were quiet for a long while, soaking in the atmosphere of the fair below them. Finally, Dane spoke.

"I'm sorry about Jimmy Sullivan. Those boys truly have no manners."

Ren was comforted by the steady rise and fall of Dane's chest and the rumble of his words under her fingers curled into the front of his shirt. She had all but forgotten about the man's unwelcome embrace in the bliss that was Dane's. Dismissing it, she shrugged.

"I swear I'll never let another person touch you without permission again. Not even me," he continued.

She tipped her head and caught the fierce protectiveness in his eyes. Though she had made the decision long ago not to allow herself to be a victim anymore, Dane clearly recognized she'd spent most of her adolescence with hands on her that she had not authorized, and she appreciated his intent. She reached up to touch his jaw lightly and smiled at him.

"You know you're always welcome."

It was true, she'd never seen the side of Dane at the ranch that she'd seen tonight when he'd taken hold of the Sullivan boy. She'd been just about sure he would hit Jimmy but as he always did, he'd shown restraint, and she had no fears he would ever turn on her. The man had the patience of Job and she'd seen him time and time again gently correct a colt until it made the right decision, never losing his cool. He was human, she was sure, but when it counted most, he kept his head.

His protective gaze dissolved into something different; that storm she had seen in his eyes when she'd first arrived at the Baylor ranch was present again.

"Ren, I..." He stopped, choosing his words carefully. "I saw red when I saw Jimmy touching you. I want to be the only one whose touch you welcome. I want to be the one you come to when you need anything. Nobody has ever made me feel the things you make me feel."

She hung on his every word, her fingers still cupping his stubbled jaw as they crested the highest precipice of the ferris wheel's trajectory. "What does it feel like?"

He reached across them, slid his hand over her neck, under her hair and took her mouth just as they started the downward journey at the ride's full speed. The sudden drop in altitude made her stomach flutter and he claimed the kiss with every emotion laid bare. The intensity of his kiss combined with gravity made her breathless in the best way possible. Every cell felt like it wanted to implode and burn at the same time and her heart felt like it would burst clear out of her chest.

~

The ride made a full rotation before Dane pulled away from Ren. She had shuffled across the seat, as close as she could get to him. He wanted her even closer but common decency didn't allow it. Heart thundering wildly, he used the arm across her shoulders to draw her tighter to him and swallowed. He was as close as he'd ever come to loving someone and he was pretty sure he'd crossed right over that threshold into the foreign territory without even realizing it. It scared the shit out of him.

TWENTY

THE VIEW OF the sunrise from the front porch double rocker of the Baylor family home was about the prettiest thing Ren had ever seen. She curled in closer to Dane's chest, taking a sip of her coffee. He tucked the soft white blanket they were wrapped in tighter around her shoulders and gave her a squeeze. She was still in her pajamas but he was dressed for the day, stealing the last few moments from what had been a magical night. Gage and Kerri had stayed over at Ella and Caine's and they had taken full advantage of it as if they were a pair of newlyweds on their honeymoon. Ren made a mental note to pick up the trail of clothing from the kitchen to Dane's bedroom before the kids got home.

"Much as I hate to do it, I gotta get to the barn." Dane spoke but didn't make any movement toward departure.

"Mmm."

They sat in silence for a couple moments longer.

"Your mama knows about us, doesn't she?" Ren had had a suspicion but it was primarily because Ella sent them back to the ranch without the kids; she was reasonably sure Ella was aware of what was going on with Dane.

When he didn't reply right away, Ren looked up at him and caught a guilty expression on his handsome features.

"She knew. Hell, according to her, half of Three Rivers knows, they're just too polite to say it," he teased.

"What does Ella say? Does she think I'm a terrible person?" Ren had stopped caring what her own mother thought of her, but Dane's mother was different. Ella had befriended her, made her feel at home, and the thought that she might feel betrayed or think less of Ren because of her relationship with Dane—well, it bothered her.

"She says she wants you to bring her a basket of tomatoes from your garden when they get ripe."

Ren frowned.

"Seriously? Your mother finds out you're sleeping with the help and all she says is she wants a basket of tomatoes from my garden?"

Dane's jaw tightened at the same time his grip on Ren loosened.

"You *know* that's not what this is."

Ren sat up, squared him in her sights.

"No, *I* know that's not what this is, but technically, that is *exactly* what this is, and that is what other people will think that it is. You *are* sleeping with the help."

She could tell she had ruffled Dane's feathers, could almost see him bristling. She felt bad but after last night, she knew they were about to cross a line they couldn't uncross and she wanted to make sure he had considered every option. At the same time, it might have been her last ditch effort to protect herself before she gave her heart up completely to this man.

"To hell with what other people think."

"I agree." Ren hadn't noticed Finn come out of the house until he spoke. He walked out onto the porch and Dane made no move to let her go—in fact, tightened his grip on her again.

"Oh hell, he knows too?" Ren rolled her eyes. "Am I the only person who still thinks this is a secret?"

"Relax, he never came out and said it in so many words." Finn took off his hat and ran a hand through his dark hair. "Well, he *did* tell me I couldn't ask you on a date. But that could have been a 'no fraternizing in the workplace' policy reminder."

Ren looked at Dane, who shrugged, and still made no move to get out of the rocker.

"You two are thick as thieves. You'd have to be a blind man not to see that *something* is going on beyond raising that little boy—which you're doing a hell of a job with, by the way."

"You didn't come out here to commend our parenting skills, Finn," Dane said.

"No, I came out here to see where the hell you were, the cattle are starving." Finn laughed. "But... I also overheard some of your conversation and I just wanna say that life is way too short not to spend it with someone who makes you happy. And to be proud of that. Take them out and show them off. And to hell with what anyone thinks, as long as you're happy.

"There were a lot of things Sunny and I did when she was sick that made a lot of people talk. They didn't think a girl as sick as she was should be out and about like she was. Truth is, people get all hung up on the 'shoulds' and 'shouldn'ts' in life and they forget to actually live that life—and by the time they realize it, it's too late.

"So maybe a sick girl shouldn't barrel race or Dane shouldn't be canoodling with his homemaker, but if it's what you feel in your heart and it makes you happy, then that's exactly what you *should* do."

Ren hadn't noticed but while his brother had been speaking, Dane had tightened his hold on her so much she could barely breathe. He had snugged her up tight against his torso and she could almost feel his heart beating.

Finn put his hat back on and scuffed the sole of his boot against the porch. "I know it's none of my business, and I don't know much about how to fix people's problems, but this is something I know way too well. You don't get to do it over, so do it right the first time, and to hell with what everyone else thinks."

The last sentence he directed at Dane, and

Ren could feel the emotion between the brothers. They had clearly seen one another through a lot.

Carefully, Ren extricated herself from Dane's arms and rose, wrapping her arms around Finn. He hesitated a moment and then hugged her back. She kissed his cheek, let him go, and hoped all her gratitude had been apparent in her hug.

TWENTY-ONE

DANE FINISHED IN the barn, passing the kids riding their bikes in the yard. Gage was getting the best mileage he could out of his arm since his cast had been removed that very morning, and it made Dane smile. He watched Kerri stop to send a text message on her cell phone while Gage steered jubilant circles around her.

He took the steps into the house two at a time, eager to have a minute alone with Ren in the daylight. With Ella and Finn in the know, they'd all but announced their situation to his family but they were still working out how to tell the kids, so they were still strictly boss and employee when it came to Gage and Kerri.

Ren was at the kitchen sink, slicing strawberries into a colander and keeping a close eye on the kids through the window overlooking the yard. He slipped his arms around her waist from behind and drew her close to him, pressing a light kiss to her neck.

"You know, when school starts next month, Kerri isn't going to have as much time for Gage... I'm glad things happened this way, so they have some time to spend together and build a good relationship." She spoke with a smile, tipping her head to permit Dane better access to her flesh but not taking her eyes off of the children.

"Well, Gage will be starting up, too, so he'll be making new friends... and that will give us a little more time to ourselves." Dane punctuated his words with soft kisses along her shoulder. He felt her shift back against him almost imperceptibly and noted that while she still held a paring knife and strawberry in hand, she had stopped slicing. He smiled, pleased at the reactions he could draw from her.

A week had passed since Finn had found him all wrapped up in Ren on the front porch. Finn had never been a particularly eloquent man but he seemed to know what he was talking about and it did something for Ren's feelings that Dane hadn't been able to figure out. She seemed freer, somehow.

Eventually, they would go public but for now, he was enjoying the little bubble they had to themselves, learning the nuances of one another's personalities and bodies. She hadn't slept in her bed all week. Oh, she always convinced Kerri she was going to bed in her own room but he'd hear her creeping down the stairs not ten minutes later. He'd pull back the sheets, open his arms, and not let go of her until his alarm woke them. She'd get up and go back up the stairs to her bed, to emerge a couple of hours later to wake the kids.

They were careful during the day, managing to steal kisses, touches, and desire- fueled looks that culminated when they finally came together at night. The days seemed that much longer when he couldn't get the taste or feel of her out of his mind. Soon, he would tell Gage that Ren wasn't just his nanny.

"So... what do you say about a date?" He spoke against the soft spot behind her ear, his hands sliding just inside of the hem of her shirt to touch her warm skin.

Ren raised an eyebrow and craned her neck to look at him.

"A date, eh? How do you propose we manage that one?"

He smiled, gave her a little squeeze.

"I was just thinking we could pack a lunch and ride up to check a few fences in the South pasture."

"And what would we do with Kerri and Gage?"

He looked over her shoulder out at the kids, resting his chin there, his cheek pressed against hers and shrugged a little.

"We'll set them up in front of a movie with snacks. Kerri's old enough to mind Gage for a couple of hours and Finn is only a couple hundred feet away in the guest house if anything happens."

When she didn't immediately respond, he gave her another encouraging squeeze.

"Come on, this is your boss telling you to take an afternoon off. With me. They'll be fine. They won't even notice we're gone."

Finally, a smile spread over her features as she warmed to the idea.

"You go saddle up and I'll fix a couple of sandwiches."

~

Ren worked quickly, pulling together a pretty impressive cold lunch for their picnic and ushering the kids into the living room in front of one of the latest animated hits with a bowl full of popcorn and a promise that they wouldn't be long.

"I'm just going to help your uncle Dane with the stock," she promised Gage, who gave her a big hug. She kissed him amiably on top of the head. The truth was this child had weaseled his way into her heart with very little effort at all. It was difficult, at times, not to imagine them as one big family.

"We'll probably even be back before the movie is over." Ren straightened, ruffled Kerri's hair playfully. The teen had her nose stuck in her phone, sending another text message. "Ker. The boy in front of you, not the one in the phone." She tipped her head, raising the best stern eyebrow she could muster. "If you need anything, you know Uncle Finn is just down the yard, and his number is right by the phone, okay?"

Both nodded dutifully but Kerri was still focused on tapping words into the screen of her phone and Gage had already started double fisting the popcorn as the opening credits of the movie began to roll.

"Be good. Love yous."

She headed for the barn with Dane's saddle bags packed full of sandwiches and fruit and a bottle of wine to find him with Maverick all tacked up and Roxy just about ready. He smiled when he saw her, took the saddle bags away from her, swinging them over his shoulder and tucked his fingers into her belt loops. He pulled her to him for a brief, tight moment, pressing a firm kiss to her lips.

"Kids all settled?"

She nodded, thinking of Gage's excitement to be left with Kerri. She was, after all, old enough to babysit, and Gage so enjoyed spending time with her.

"Movie was started, popcorn was being consumed. We have at least a couple hours before they send the search party out looking for us."

Ren couldn't help the giddy flip-flop of excitement in her stomach as Dane released her and she watched him tie the saddlebags onto Maverick. This was almost thrilling—a broad expanse of time stretching out ahead of them where they could do nothing but focus on one another. They led the horses out of the barn and Dane gave her a leg up onto Roxy's back, patting her backside as she went. She gave him a mockingly indignant look. It was almost as though they were a normal, everyday couple.

Clearly picking up that it was a leisurely ride, not one with any real intent for work, Roxy and Maverick ambled along side by side, close enough that Dane could reach out and take Ren's hand as they headed for the upper pasture. He entwined his fingers through hers.

"I was thinking..."

"That's never a good sign." She teased, giving his hand a squeeze, her heart full to bursting. The day was warm, the sun high. A soft breeze stirred the nearly grown hay fields to their left. And the man riding beside her was as delighted to spend an afternoon with her as she was with him.

"Do you suppose we should invite my folks over for dinner?"

She raised a brow.

"You know your family is welcome for dinner anytime... you just have to give me a heads up so I can make enough food to feed everyone."

His pointed look made her realize she wasn't quite on the right track.

"I meant *we* host them. Together. Give them a heads up about what's going on. Tell Gage and Kerri..." He chuckled, gave her hand another squeeze. "I don't want you to feel uncomfortable... but I think we shouldn't have to hide this, anymore."

Though she yearned to be able to go to town with him, rest her head on his shoulder in his pick-up truck, hold his hand in public, the nagging voice inside of her that said she'd just be hurting him a little farther down the road piped up, insistent.

That voice had been quiet for days now—since Finn's inspiring speech, so she was surprised to hear it pop up.

"Are you sure that's what you want?"

"Wouldn't have mentioned it if I wasn't."

"Dane... you know this situation is... complicated. Once we go public, we can't undo this. When we tell Gage we're a family... if things go under, it's going to hurt him. I don't doubt you for even a second but my mother..."

"Wouldn't Three Rivers be a good place to make a final stand against your mama? With the whole Baylor clan backing you up?"

She swallowed, considering his words. If she knew it would be that easy, she would buy it, hook, line and sinker. But it couldn't be that easy. Anita was relentless. She would set up camp in Three Rivers. She would not stop until she destroyed their lives. She would hurt the Baylors because that would hurt Ren.

Ren knew that while she was strong enough to pack all of her things and spirit away in the night, force a smile for Kerri and tell her everything was okay, work whatever job she had to to help them get by, she didn't have the strength to live in the same town as the woman who had tried to kill her sister. And she didn't have the strength to stand up to her mother in a battle for legal custody of Kerri.

When it came down to the truth—she was afraid of her mother.

"You didn't ask for that. You asked for a homemaker to help with Gage, not a damaged girl with mommy issues who you would need to protect."

"I know you've been doing this on your own for a long time, sugar. But it doesn't mean you're any less strong if you have a little help."

Ren didn't respond immediately. It wasn't that she didn't want the help. It was that she had always felt like this was her own cross to bear.

"I asked for help with Gage. And look what it brought me." He gave her hand a gentle squeeze. "Ask mama, I didn't want any help in the beginning, either."

She softened a little.

"Maybe I'll never have to employ the Baylor backup."

"I bet you never will."

Just then, the cell phone in Ren's back pocket buzzed. She released Dane's hand to take Roxy's reins in the opposite one and pulled the phone out, her heart thudding, concerned it was Kerri reporting another broken arm for Gage. She didn't recognize the number on the screen but answered anyways.

"Hello?"

Silence.

Frowning, Ren looked again at the number on the screen.

"Hello? I think you have the wrong number." It was quiet, but she could tell there was someone on the other end of the line—they just weren't saying anything. "Goodbye."

Dane gave her a questioning look but she

shrugged and stuffed the phone back into her pocket.

"I shouldn't have even answered it if it wasn't Kerri. Sorry, I think it's so rude when people answer their cell phones on a date." She shook her head apologetically but Dane shrugged it off.

"Don't worry about it."

They rounded the pasture trail and found themselves approaching a huge live oak in the middle of the field.

Dane dismounted and tied off Maverick's reins so he could graze, and then helped Ren off of Roxy and untying the saddle bags. They made their way under the shade of the tree and spread out a blanket Ren had brought along, sprawling out and pulling out the cold food she had packed for them.

~

Sometime later, with their bellies full, Dane reclined with his back against the trunk of the tree. He patted his leg and Ren rested on her back with her head in his lap, her hair spread out across the denim of his jeans like a halo of fire. He put his fingers into it and smiled, resting his other hand lightly on her abdomen. He could have stayed this way for hours, days even. She had no idea how she quieted his soul. She broke the silence, smiling up at him.

"So tell me how it is that Three Rivers' most eligible bachelor is... well, still a bachelor."

He considered the question carefully.

"Just got so busy with the ranch... I knew it would be mine one day and I figured there was always time. Then the accident happened and all of a sudden, I had twice as much on my plate as before and there *wasn't* time." He supposed it was why he had seized this opportunity with Ren.

"I think it was good of you to take on Gage. I know your parents would have gladly stepped in."

"I know, but Gavin named me in the will. It was the very least I could do."

"The least you could do is pretty damn good." She covered his hand on her midsection with her own, lacing her fingers through his.

"Sometimes I don't think so. Especially before you got here. When he broke his arm, it was a pretty low point." He chuckled now, thinking of it. "It's a lot more complicated than Gavin made it look and I used to spend about three quarters of my day worrying that somebody would realize I didn't have a goddamn clue what I was doing."

"Well, I happen to think you were doing just fine when I got here." Lifting her hand to rest on the back of his neck, she shifted herself up to meet his lips for a kiss. He supported her, drawing her up so he held her against his chest, smiling against her mouth.

"I'm doing so much better now."

He took her mouth then, without apology or hesitation, drawing her flush against him. His hands burrowed under the hem of her shirt, goosebumps rising under his calloused fingertips as he stroked the silky flesh at the small of her back.

She tasted like sunshine and goodness and she felt even better. It was hard to remember now what life had felt like before she had rumbled up the dusty driveway of the ranch in that beat up Jimmy.

Ren made a soft noise against his mouth as he shifted her into his lap, straddling his waist without breaking the kiss. She cupped his stubble-dusted jaw lightly before curling her fingers into his hair and pulled back to look him in the eye with a playfully accusatory expression.

"Dane Baylor, did you bring me out into the middle of nowhere to have your way with me?"

"I'll never tell. But if that's where this is goin'..."

Ren threw her head back and laughed, and Dane joined in. It was relieving to be so free with her for what felt like the first time, without being behind closed doors. He pushed up out of his seated position and rolled her onto her back on the blanket, finding the ticklish spot on her ribs when her shirt rode up. Burying his face in her neck, his stubble scraped her and made her wriggle more. Her laugh was the best sound he'd heard in a long time, and their conversation about her mother on the ride up felt a million miles away.

TWENTY-TWO

REN LOST TRACK of the time they spent beneath the oak laughing, loving, and learning more of the intricacies of one another, and by the time they got ready to ride down off the hill, the sun had begun to head West. While Dane loaded the saddlebags onto Maverick, she shot a quick text off to let Kerri know they were on their way back and slid her phone into her pocket without a second thought.

She halfway expected to find Gage in the dooryard on his bike, but it was eerily quiet. As they dismounted, Dane took Roxy's reins and gave Ren a squeeze.

"Why don't you go tell the kids to wash up and we'll go into town for dinner. They're probably starving, and I know I sure worked up an appetite."

"Alright." Giving Roxy a pat on the neck, she headed for the house. As soon as she pushed the front door open, Ren could sense something was wrong. The house was huge, sure, but there was never this stillness to the air with a five and fifteen year old inside. Rex had been restlessly pacing on the porch and he followed her into the house, now, whining.

"What's the matter, buddy?" She ruffled the dog's ears lightly and he whined again in response. "Gage? Kerri?"

The panic that overtook her was immediate and all-consuming. Her heart rate skittered out of control as she fumbled for the phone in her back pocket and realized Kerri had not replied to her text message. The rule was to always reply. Ren picked up speed, looking into every room in the house as she called for the kids even though she knew she wouldn't find them.

It was every worst nightmare she had had over the last four years. Always, Anita found them, but never had she found Kerri alone. She usually called Ren or tracked her down outside of her job—once, she had been parked at the end of the driveway when Ren had come home from running errands. They'd always had a chance to get gone before anything bad happened. Until now. In a blind frenzy, she ran full tilt into Dane's chest as she started outside to get him. He took hold of her arms to steady her.

"I could hear you yelling from the barn. What's going on?"

Ren felt numb from head to toe. Her mind raced over every possible scenario she could think of, but it kept circling back to the obvious one: somehow, her mother had tracked them down and taken not only Kerri but now Gage, irrevocably engaging the Baylor family in the disaster that was her life. Dane had asked her a couple of times in the beginning what she was so afraid of—*this*.

"The kids are gone. I knew if we left them alone..."

"They're not just *gone*, Ren. Calm down. Take a breath." He tugged her close to his chest but she was in full flight mode and the last thing she wanted was to be held in one place. Fear ricocheted through her bloodstream, a harsh contrast to all the endorphins she'd been awash with not an hour before.

"They're not here! I checked everywhere."

"There's a whole ranch out here, sugar. They're probably with Finn."

"Dane, listen to me. We have to call the police. She's probably a hundred miles from here by now with them... oh God, and Gage. I'm so stupid, how could I think this would be okay?"

She could see his jaw tighten—for a brief moment, he might have given himself over to a panicked thought, but he controlled himself quickly, smoothing out his features. His voice was steady and soothing when he spoke again.

"If it makes you feel better, we'll call the Sheriff now... but we're just gonna have to call and cancel him when we find those kids."

She wished she could believe him as he took her hand and led her into the yard, past Gage's bike which had been haphazardly leaned against the steps. Her heart was breaking. Everything felt wrong, right down to the cellular level.

Dane finally accepted defeat after they'd checked with Finn and been through the barns. He made her sit on a bale of hay while he called the Sheriff. The conversation was short, his language more urgent than his tone betrayed. Afterward, he crouched in front of her, taking her trembling hands in his and waited until she made eye contact with him.

"We *will* find them."

Ren nodded, trying to keep her head in the game. Dane's calm demeanor seemed surreal—after all, Gage was missing, too. He didn't know Anita but from the stories she had told him, so perhaps he just didn't get how serious the whole situation was. Anita wouldn't hurt them right away. She had to sweeten Kerri up to her after years of no contact... but eventually, she would harm her. And God knew why she wanted Gage. Ren would never forgive herself if anything bad happened to that little boy.

~

Dane paced while he waited for the Sheriff to show up. Ren had gone inside with Finn but Dane couldn't quiet himself long enough to sit and he didn't want Ren to see him agitated. If anybody could handle this situation, he thought, it was Sheriff Banks Montgomery. He'd grown up practically a member of the Baylor clan and while they never had to make use of the law man's station, Dane had heard good things throughout the community about the young Sheriff.

Banks' cruiser rolled in and Dane released a breath of relief. His deputy, Carter Collins had ridden along and Dane met them at the car, shaking each man's hand in greeting.

"Banks."

"Dane, it's been too long. Shame it's under these circumstances, though."

"You're damn right." Dane sighed, shifted. "If you want to talk to Ren, she's in the house. She knows a lot more about what seems to be going on here."

"You've looked everywhere here at the ranch?"

"Just about every little nook and cranny we could think of. The James boys and Myrna and Jonas Pierce are riding the back, but we came from that way when we came in, so we would have seen them."

"We'll call in a couple more officers to help with the search, but in the meantime, I *would* like to talk to Ren. You said she believes this is an abduction?"

Dane nodded. The concept of Anita Maddock had seemed like something that couldn't touch them here in Three Rivers. Turned out maybe he had been wrong to brush off her concerns. He headed for the house with Montgomery and Collins on his heels. In what seemed like the most unnatural scenario, Finn was putting on coffee and Ren was seated at the kitchen table, her hands clasped together in front of her. He had to hand it to her—she had been near hysterics but she had reined it in and she hadn't cried a single tear. She had turned out to be every bit the strong woman he'd thought her to be when she'd first showed up.

Banks sat in the seat opposite Ren, waving away the coffee Finn offered him. Carter sat also, but Dane stood nearby, his arms crossed over his chest, overlooking the scene. He'd tried more than once to put his arms around Ren and comfort her but that didn't seem to be what she wanted so he settled for being near if she needed him.

In truth, he could have used her soft touch for comfort, too. He had no idea what Anita would want with Gage or why she would have taken the boy. His stomach roiled with the idea of anything bad happening to his nephew while his mind tried over and over to convince him they were just playing hide and seek in the hay mow—even though they'd checked there a dozen times.

Finn busied himself putting on a second pot of coffee while Dane listened as Collins and Montgomery questioned Ren. He took a moment to consider the options. Ren was afraid of this woman—she'd told him about the things Anita had done to her and Kerri—what was stopping her from harming Gage? For the first time, and just for a brief moment, he regretted not heeding Ren's warnings. She had tried to tell him half a dozen times Anita would cause problems down the road but he hadn't believed her, and now Gage could pay the price for his uncle's stupidity. It was every fear about failing as the child's guardian that he had ever had.

But heeding Ren's warnings would have meant no Ren. Strong, soft, giving, beautiful Ren. Who, even now, when she should be panicking, answered every question Banks asked with dignity—even the ones that irritated Dane with their redundancy. Ren, who had lit up his life when he didn't even realize how badly he needed the sunshine. And Kerri. The pair clearly needed the safe haven that had been the Baylor ranch. In the short time they'd been there, he'd seen both of them blossom, and Gage, too, and was proud he was a part of it.

No, he wouldn't have sacrificed what he had in his life now to avoid the potential to get hurt. If there was one thing the Baylors had learned well through losing first Gavin and June, then Sunny, it was that you couldn't let the fear of being hurt stop you from loving. At the end of the day, even if you didn't have two red cents to rub together, you'd still be rich if you had a little love in your life.

Dane shifted, moving closer to the kitchen table and dropping a hand on Ren's shoulder. He gave it a supportive squeeze.

Banks shifted back in his seat.

"I think we should move this questioning down to the station." Pushing his chair back, first the sheriff and then his deputy rose. Ren jumped to her feet.

"Where are your mama and daddy?" Banks asked Dane.

"I called them just before I called you. They're with Noah closing up the shop but we'll let them know to meet us down at the station."

The four of them filed out of the Baylor house, leaving Finn behind to tie up loose ends.

Dane helped Ren into the passenger side of his pick up the way he always did. When she flinched away from the hand he tried to put on her knee as they pulled out the lane of the ranch, he frowned, tightening his grip on the steering wheel.

"Look, if you think I'm gonna let you just go off into the woods and lick your wounds alone, you don't know much about me." It was hard not to feel shirked when he was hurting too. There was a whole other layer to the pain and anxiety she was dealing with, though. No doubt she was reliving scenes of abuse and neglect with the sore topic of her mother all dredged up.

When he glanced over, she was staring straight ahead, her eyes filled up with tears.

"Sugar..." He reached out for her hand. "I didn't mean to be..."

"I never meant for this to happen, Dane." She put her hand into his and the grip she took could have choked a turkey.

"I know you didn't."

"I didn't come here to Three Rivers to find some well-off cowboy and turn his life upside down. I came here to get away from Anita. And I couldn't even do that right."

Dane squeezed her hand in return.

"Nobody thinks this happened on purpose,

Ren."

"I should never have replied to your ad."

Frowning, Dane pulled the truck over and shifted into park. He unbuckled his seat belt and reached across to unbuckle Ren's. With little effort, he tugged her across the seat into what the boys all called the 'girlfriend seat' and into his arms.

"Stop trying to talk yourself out of this. Stop trying to talk *me* out of you. It ain't gonna happen. Even if you had been a waitress or bagging my groceries at Sawyer's, I would have found you."

She sniffed, but no tears had spilled yet. He tipped her chin up with one finger.

"Don't think for one second, Ren Maddock, that you are anywhere except exactly where you need to be. We will get through this, we'll find the kids, and we will hire every lawyer in the country to make sure your mother can't ever bother you again if we have to. Got it?"

She gave him a long look before she finally nodded and nestled into his side.

TWENTY-THREE

AFTER BANKS HAD finished his questioning, Ren sat with Dane on a bank of hard seats at the sheriff's office, waiting. It felt wrong to go back to the ranch and sit on their thumbs now that the investigation had been taken over by the sheriff and the biggest hub of activity was here.

The longer they stayed here, however, the worse she felt. Now that they had turned it over to the sheriff, it was real—her mother was a suspect—no matter how far she'd gone to get away from her, it wasn't far enough. She had been foolish to believe there was any safety to be had in Three Rivers, or anywhere else. Dane had convinced her, made her feel wanted, comfortable, and safe. She'd become complacent, and now she wasn't the only one paying the price.

There was no room for them to pretend nothing was happening between them with the urgency that filled the air and he had her tucked tightly against his side, as if he could transfer the strength and patience he had to her, if he had any left. She was sure he was roiling with the same sick feeling inside. She couldn't understand how he was managing to hold himself together when all she wanted to do was surrender to the flurry of feelings coursing through her. Anger, resentment, panic, giving in to any one of them would have been a relief. Carefully managing herself the way she was now was agony.

Banks emerged from his office, beckoning Dane, and he gave Ren an encouraging squeeze before he rose to greet his old friend. He shook the sheriff's hand with a firm grip and cast a glance over his shoulder at Ren, his mask of calm cracking just a moment as she noticed worry knitting his handsome features for the first time.

The rest of the Baylor clan arrived then. The sight of them made her feel even more ill - she wished for the hundredth time she hadn't brought trouble to the doorstep of this family who had been nothing but endlessly kind and open to her. She wouldn't have blamed a single one of them for hating her but they circled her immediately, Ella the first to close her in a tight hug. She could read the worry for Gage etched on the faces of these people she'd come to love, but they were still concerned about her.

"I'm so..."

Caine cut her off.

"Sorry is for when the bad stuff is over and there ain't another thing we can do."

Though she hadn't shed a single tear at that point, Ren's eyes were dangerously full at his words. He was the same kind of gentle, patient, masterful man that he had raised his son to be. She didn't deserve their kindness.

"Listen, sweetheart. There ain't a single one of us in this whole room who hasn't had troubles in life that ended up spilling over on someone else by accident," he continued.

She could see by the nods from Finn and Noah that they concurred. Of course everybody had regrets and made mistakes that affected others, but Ren was convinced hers went well beyond the threshold of what was reasonably acceptable.

Dane returned to the group, his face not betraying whether there had been good news or bad news.

"There's not much to go on yet, but local police went by Anita's house and she's not there... Which could mean she's at work, not that she's halfway across the country." He shrugged, reached for Ren's hand and drew her close. "They are going to try running her credit card in the system and see if there's been any activity."

Ren let out a long breath and tried to swallow but her mouth was dry with fear at the thought of confirming their worst nightmare. She knew it in her heart, but hearing them confirm, out loud, Anita was here and had taken the kids would be a hard blow.

Ushering the group to a long line of hard plastic chairs, Dane put an arm over Ren's shoulders and held her tight. Though Noah raised a brow, the expression Dane shot him shut down any questioning. Now was not the time.

A flurry of activity in the portion of the office that contained all of the desks drew her attention abruptly and the whole family leapt to their feet.

Banks exited his office quietly, nodding to a couple of officers preparing to go to their cars and approached the Baylors. His voice was quiet and tight—he was a man who spent his lifetime delivering bad news and he had clearly learned to manage himself to incite the least amount of panic.

"We got a hit on her credit card at a motel just a few miles from here." Ren's heart clenched at his words. Had her mother been right behind them this whole time? Had she ever been truly safe?

~

Dane stepped forward. "Which hotel?"

Banks shot an exasperated look at Dane. When he'd first started into law enforcement, he'd done his best to recruit the eldest Baylor boy— they'd been such close friends growing up, it only made sense to keep the peace in Three Rivers together after they'd raised so much hell as teenagers. Dane had chosen the ranch and never looked back.

"Not a chance, Baylor." Rarely did Banks pull this authoritative voice on Dane—rarely did he need to, the Baylors were an upstanding family in the community. Because of their friendship, the sheriff clearly wanted to keep the family in the loop but knew the dangers of having a civilian on scene at what could turn into a terse standoff. Dane had ridden along with him a handful of times, but writing speeding tickets was a far cry from dealing with an abduction case—especially one that his friend was so close to. "I'll go, and that's the next best thing. But the lot of you," he gestured to the family, including Ren, "are staying right here, and Deputy Collins is going to make sure of that."

Cursing quietly under his breath, Dane turned to Ren. She looked fragile now, a shell of the strong woman who had been holding his household together all summer, and it made Dane uneasy. There had been days she plunged headfirst into ranch chores he had been sure would have scared any other woman away, but she had been fearless. He had wondered if anything could affect her, and here they had found it. In one all-too-short afternoon, the world had drilled to the root of her weaknesses and exposed every one to the open air.

"He's right, honey. We'd be useless, and he's practically an honorary Baylor. It'll be alright." Ella interjected, ever the voice of reason and cohesive bond in their family. "There's nothing any of us can do that Banks can't do ten times over."

Ella guided her son and Ren back to the chairs along the wall. They were meant for criminals in for booking, not anxious families, but asking everyone to go home would be futile. Dane recognized Ella's motives - the best she could do was try to manage the anxiety and panic in the room, and that was how she would manage her own. She had spent a lot of time organizing and guiding the Baylor family and she knew how to do it with efficiency and precision. No matter who else thought they were the boss at any given time, it was always Ella. His mother was the backbone of the family.

She dispatched Finn and Noah to acquire coffee, 'and not the stuff from the machine here', and then she and her husband flanked Dane and Ren in the seats, offering their physical presence as a balm as they settled in for a long wait.

TWENTY-FOUR

IT WASN'T AN hour later that Deputy Collins ushered the family into Sheriff Montgomery's office, arranging them in the small space carefully. The Sheriff was nowhere in sight so Ren could only assume, hopefully, this was a safety precaution and they were bringing Anita in. Though they'd displayed an exponential amount of restraint, she was certain the Baylors were not the type to let themselves be done wrong, especially this badly, without a little bit of bad blood.

She could hear a commotion in the hallway outside and winced, causing Dane to tighten his grip on her hand.

"They must have them, sugar. They're just fine."

Banks entered his office not long after, removed his hat and took up a spot not behind the desk but sitting on the edge of it.

"We've got them..." His face clearly showed he

had some conflict.

"Can we see them?" Ren's heart thundered in her chest with anticipation. All she really needed to do was lay her hands on her sister and make sure she was okay physically. Any mental damage her mother had done to her could be repaired later.

"Of course. But I need you to stay, Ren, afterward. We need to have a talk."

Ren could hardly think straight, but Dane nodded to his friend and helped her to her feet. The family filed out of the office to find Kerri in the hall with Gage clinging tightly to her hand.

"Ren!" Kerri's voice broke in a sob as the pair of them ran toward her. She pulled Kerri into her arms tightly and Gage wound his arms around her leg tearfully. The Baylor family moved in on them, surrounding them in a tight, loving circle. Moving from one to the other, Ren pushed first Kerri's, then Gage's hair back from their faces and gave each one a kiss before Dane swept Gage up into one arm and drew Kerri and Ren into the other. Relief, the rush of tension leaving her heart, left Ren feeling weak and she was glad to have the little family they had become over the summer so close to her.

"You guys are okay? You're all in one piece?" Ren was breathless with gratitude to see they seemed generally unharmed. Kerri swallowed tears and nodded solemnly before Ren crushed her against her chest again, her lips close to her sister's ears. "Did she say anything to you? Did she hurt you? Did she hurt Gage?"

Kerri shook her head.

"She told us she was taking us on a trip. Gage wasn't even scared until the cops showed up. She yelled a lot, then. I... I'm sorry, Ren. I thought it was a boy texting me and he was gonna come over and visit."

"It's okay, Kerri. It doesn't matter." Ren didn't even know how to begin to probe for the emotional scarring her mother could have inflicted. She could deal with that later. For now, holding her sister in her arms was the sweetest thing she'd felt. "I'm so sorry. I will find a way to make sure this can never happen again."

Banks stood back for about ten minutes, giving them some time to reconnect before he summoned Ren again. When Dane tried to follow, he shook his head at his friend, suggesting instead that Dane get everyone organized to head home. There would be child protective services and psychological exams to deal with, he told them, but they could wait until the family had a chance to absorb the children back into their unit.

Sitting again on the edge of his desk, Ren looked up at Banks Montgomery and wondered if he ever sat behind it. He was a personable enough man and Dane and the Baylors trusted him so she felt she could, too.

"Ren, we can detain your mother for the abduction of Gage Baylor, but... there is an issue of custody here that we need to address."

Ren's heart dropped nearly to her toes. She had known this day would come—when someone would question why her sister, a minor, lived with her when she didn't have legal custody. Kerri had been moved around enough that the schools didn't question when Ren signed homework or attended parent teacher interviews in the lieu of their 'very busy, entrepreneurial mother'. In the beginning, she had feared if she didn't move quickly enough, spiriting Kerri away, her sister would slip through the cracks into the broken foster system if the abuse was reported and she sought custody. Not that she would have ever been able to afford the lawyers and advisers necessary. Not that she could now.

She anxiously twisted her hands in her lap, considering her next words. She had to be careful.

"What did she tell you?"

"She told me you kidnapped Kerri four years ago and she's been searching for you ever since."

None of that was a lie. It was hard to say if her mother was in her right mind or not, considering that she'd not only taken Kerri, but a second child she didn't even know from the Baylor ranch. Anita had cut straight to the bone here.

Ren wished then that Dane had been allowed to come into the office with her. She'd been strong for four damn years and now he'd made her need him. She'd given him some of her heavy burden to bear but suddenly she was on her own again.

"I did take her."

"Why?"

Ren's jaw tightened, her eyes dropping. She'd always told the truth to the law, that was how her daddy had raised her—that truth was the most important thing. She'd lied by omission more than a couple times since she'd taken Kerri and she'd fudged the truth when it came to schools and work experience by necessity but when it mattered, she told the truth. But here, the truth hurt. It meant opening up wounds that wouldn't only be visible to someone she didn't know, but they would be investigated, probed, ripped open wider than they were before. Nonetheless, she opted for the truth.

"She was hurting my sister, like she hurt me for years."

Banks raised a brow, inclining his head toward Ren. This was a new development for him.

"Is there any record of abuse?"

Ren shook her head resolutely. There were a lot of reasons she hadn't told, ranging from worrying about foster care to not wanting anyone's pity.

Crossing his arms over his chest, the sheriff leaned back on his desk and let out a tight, pent up breath.

"That would have made this whole process a hell of a lot easier."

"I was always afraid we'd end up in a group home or the foster system..." Ren shrugged. She felt like a helium balloon with most of the air let out of it, floating just inches off the floor, but much too weak to maintain equilibrium.

"That's often the way. Fear. And it's a damn shame." He rose, moving toward the door. "For now, Anita said Kerri can stay with you. It *is* likely, because of everything with Gage, she will be incarcerated for a period of time... but technically, she still has legal custody of your sister, Ren. I think you would be wise to lawyer up. Right now. Or this will happen again, and I don't think anybody here wants that to happen."

Ren could barely contain the wash of relief that came over her when Banks finally walked past her and opened the door, signaling she could go. Dane stood just outside of the door, as if he'd been poised there the whole time, waiting for her.

He drew her up in his arms as if the fact that they had been apart had been the only thing that had mattered. His lips against her hair comforted her. She was exhausted, as if she'd run a marathon.

"I need a lawyer..."

"I know," he murmured fiercely. "But let's get you *home*, first."

~

Even Dane had to admit the short drive home from the station was agonizing. He drove as quickly as he dared, his hand resting on Ren's knee as a gesture of support, moving it only to shift gears. His mind darted over the day's events and compiled a list of things yet to be done; the sun was setting quickly. He'd need to call the family's lawyer right away, and he was sure, since Finn and Noah had both been at the sheriff's office with him all afternoon, the chores were yet to be done. But most of all, he wanted to get them both back to the ranch so he could put the girls and Gage together in his arms again. This was *his* family. He hadn't felt so complete in ages.

Beside him, Ren was almost catatonic. He could hardly stand it.

"What's on your mind, sugar?" He knew it was the wrong question as soon as it crossed his lips. What *wasn't* on her mind? It was a loaded question at best, cruel at worst. He had no idea what they'd talked about in Banks' office, but he suspected it was what had sapped the life right out of her eyes.

Ren pursed her lips, her hands resting twisted up in her lap. Her body so still it was unnerving, as if her whole being was in physical pain and moving would be excruciating.

"I need to talk to her."

"Kerri?"

"Anita."

"Do you think..."

"I need to know why. Why would she want Kerri so badly now when I caught her trying to *kill* her four years ago? If she hated us so much, how sadistic is she to follow us for the last four years instead of just saying good riddance and being thankful she didn't have to give two shits about us anymore? She doesn't *want* to be Kerri's mother and she hasn't been mine for a long time so what the hell is wrong with her?"

Dane couldn't answer that question, couldn't even begin to understand what would drive Anita to follow the girls across the country if she hated them so much after Ren's father had passed away. He didn't understand families harbored ill will against one another, held grudges and intentionally harmed others to whom they were tied by blood-- but then, he'd never been a part of a family like that. The Baylors were a tight-knit clan that worked together as much like a community as a family. When one needed help, the rest rallied around them without question, knowing if the roles reversed, the same would be done for them. He wanted Ren to feel that support structure, alien as it was. She needed his family just as badly as he needed her.

He was quiet for a moment, gave her knee a squeeze.

"I don't know, Ren. I suspect she's the only one who knows any of that stuff. I'll talk to Banks and see if we can make it happen. I suppose you're her next of kin so that may grant you some visiting rights." He could feel Ren's body relax minutely under his hand and breathed a prayer of thanks. They had a long battle ahead of them no matter which way you sliced it, but she'd been wound tight as a spring and it was late—they both needed some sleep.

Pulling into the drive, Dane could see both the house and barn were lit up in the waning daylight. His father's pickup and Noah's Jeep both added to the collection of vehicles in the yard. The family had activated just the way he thought they would, circling the wagons to help and support those in need. He hoped Ren would learn to accept the help that was sure to come.

When she'd found the kids missing, Ren's first instinct was to track Kerri down, hit the road running and not look back with her sister in tow. When it came down to fight or flight for the last four years, she'd picked flight every time. It was old habit. With Dane's warm hand closed around her knee, his steady presence riding in the driver's seat next to her, she had made up her mind that she could fight—with him beside her, she knew she could try.

As they pulled up to the big house, she could see Kerri on the front steps, in the same shorts and tee she'd been wearing this morning. Rex was pacing around her feet and much to his dismay, Kerri was ignoring him. She was anxiously jiggling her legs and got to her feet the second Dane put the car in park, racing across the yard to hug her sister again.

"Are you okay?" Kerri's voice was frantic.

"Shouldn't *I* be asking *you* that question?" Ren could almost feel a laugh rise up in her and she again held her sister at arm's length and did another quick inventory that all of her parts were there.

"When the sheriff kept you, I thought they were going to put you in jail, too. I would have been all alone."

Dane put a hand on Ren's shoulder.

"We aren't going to let that happen."

Ren hoped he was telling the truth, because

that was the story she was going with. She hated to tell Kerri everything would be okay when it wouldn't; she had always been straight with her sister and she didn't want to stop now.

"No, we're not going to let it happen. We'll get things straightened out tomorrow, I promise. Did you eat anything?" She turned the younger girl back toward the house.

"Ella is making spaghetti."

"Sounds good to me."

~

Several hours later, with Kerri and Gage in bed and their bellies full, Ren and Dane sat across from Ella Baylor in the big house's living room. Noah and Finn had returned to their own homes and Caine had gone back into town to secure the shop for the night. Ella and Caine would be spending the night at the ranch, she had told Ren, so everybody could breathe a little easier. Considering all the trouble Ren had brought them, she wondered why the older woman didn't just kick them to the curb. Maybe she was about to deliver the blow.

She sat close to Dane, nestled against his side like it was the most natural thing in the world. It felt the safest, that was for sure. They still hadn't addressed the relationship that had developed between them with his family and the Baylors seemed to understand it was probably the least important thing happening right now.

"Tell me." Ella's voice was gentle but firm, and made Ren think the quiet guidance she saw in Dane every day when he worked with the horses came from his mother. She wanted to tell Ella because it was the easiest, most right-feeling thing to do, not because the woman demanded it.

It took the better part of an hour for Ren to lay the whole story out, from her father's passing to their arrival in Three Rivers, and then Ella knew the rest, because she'd been a part of it. All but the part where Ren had fallen in love with Ella's son.

The older woman's eyes had glazed over with tears on more than one occasion, but she'd recomposed herself by the time the story ended up in the laundromat where Ren had seen Dane's ad looking for a homemaker. With a hand clasped to her throat, the matriarch of the Baylor family deferred to her eldest son.

"So you're calling the lawyer." It wasn't so much a question as a statement.

"First thing in the morning. And Myrna Pierce. I thought with her having worked with social services for so long, she might be able to give us a little extra insight to this custody thing."

"Neighbor and long-time friend," Ella advised Ren, recognizing her slightly confused expression.

"Any little bit helps," Ren nodded.

"The most important part in all of this is making sure this family," Ella's next gesture indicated the household, including Ren and Kerri, "stays together."

TWENTY-FIVE

REN TOOK ONE deep breath and then another in an attempt to quell the nervous stomach that was now rising up her throat and threatening to come out in vomit. She hadn't spoken to her mother in years, and now with all of this additional bad blood and distance between them, she couldn't imagine it would be any easier.

It had been hard enough to talk to Anita *before* her father's death but afterward, it was nearly impossible. She was one of two Anita's at that point—either entirely despondent and non-responsive or volatile and aggressive. Ren could have lived with the quietness of her mother's depression but it was the tiptoeing on eggshells around a volatile Anita that ended up pushing Ren out of the house just weeks before her high school graduation. She wanted to stay close, for Kerri, and visited as frequently as she could stomach until she made her move and took her sister.

Sheriff Montgomery appeared in the hallway in front of her and cleared his throat to wake Ren from her trance.

"She's ready."

Ren had asked Dane not to come along. He was already behind on everything at the ranch but further—if she couldn't have Kerri with her, the only person she felt her sister was safe with was him. Anything she could do to avoid exposing her sister to the toxicity of their mother was the least she could do.

The late afternoon sun cast long shadows of window blinds on the floors of the sheriff's department. They had been here early this morning to finish taking statements from the kids, recognizing that the previous day had been long and exhausting for everyone involved. They had confirmed that Anita had tracked down Kerri's cell phone number and had been texting under the guise of being a teen aged boy in Three Rivers who had seen her at one of the gymkhana days Dane had taken the kids to. Kerri, appreciating the attention, had fallen hook, line and sinker and revealed the house address. After that, it had just been a matter of Anita waiting until the adults were gone to make her move.

Through all of this, however, they maintain that Anita had not committed a crime against Ren or Kerri, and that was the loophole through which the sheriff had been able to admit Ren to speak to her mother this afternoon.

With trepidation, Ren rose and followed

Banks down a hall to a small room. Deputy Collins was standing in a corner and in the middle of the room, handcuffed to a small table, sat Anita Maddock. Ren hadn't truly laid eyes on her in long enough that her appearance was a shock.

Her wild mahogany hair had frizzed into a halo around a gaunt face, over plucked eyebrows, injected lips. She'd lost probably forty pounds since Ren had last seen her. Altogether, she looked like a different woman with only one exception. Her eyes held the same all-consuming, jealous expression they always had.

Ren kept her distance for a few moments, hesitantly standing several feet behind the chair that had been seated across the table from her mother. As so many times before in the last twenty four hours, her instinct told her to run, but she stamped it down, along with the bile that rose in her throat.

Letting a long breath out through her nose, she pulled the chair back with a scrape and sat herself on the edge of it, poised for a quick departure if necessary. A litany of questions and accusations stormed her brain, threatening to tumble over her tongue but those, too, she held at bay, waiting. Her mother finally broke the silence.

"Ren, sweetheart." Though her word choice was clearly an attempt at endearment, her tone gave away her disdain.

"Anita." She addressed the woman formally, the time to call her 'mom' had expired with each unkind word and act of physical harm her mother had inflicted on her over the years.

"Oh sweetie, you know I prefer you to call me mama."

Her confidence bolstered by her mother's fine form, Ren relaxed just an iota. This sharp, difficult Anita was a familiar one; one she could handle. She ignored the other woman's comment and straightened, preparing for the rest of the conversation.

Anita leaned forward across the table, narrowing Ren in her sights.

"Why are you here?"

"Shouldn't I be asking *you* that question?" Ren resisted the urge to laugh.

"I missed you... wanted to try to make things right."

This time, a short burst of laughter did escape Ren and she leaned back in her chair, shaking her head and crossing her arms over her chest.

"You've always been a terrible liar."

There was a time when Ren had believed every lie Anita had said, desperate for a mother who cared for her, loved her the way a mother was supposed to. It had not been the short trip down the long flight of stairs that had sent Ren running from the house so many years ago, but the tearful apology that came after. Anita loved her, she was sorry. Ren had finally reconciled that the physical and emotional abuse spoke volumes to the contrary.

"Really, Anita... why now? When you were so desperate to get rid of Kerri the last time I saw you that you tried to kill her?"

The older woman looked momentarily flummoxed by Ren's onslaught, but regained her footing easily.

"All I want is to be close to my daughters. A mother can want that, can't she?" It was almost theatrical the way she carefully composed her eyebrows to knit together, tears welling up in her eyes, ever the victim.

"A *mother* can want those things, but you haven't been a real mother in a very long time."

"You aren't her mother, either."

These were the words that finally stung Ren. Every part of her life for the last four years had revolved around keeping Kerri safe, providing for her, and raising her into the young woman she'd become so proud of.

"That's true." It wouldn't make any difference to argue this point with Anita, because she could go down a road bearing the burden of proof and neither one of them would enjoy visiting parent teacher meetings filled with excuses, a whole week's wages spent on clothes Kerri would only outgrow a couple of months later, 'the talk' about her sister's changing body and recurring nightmares of cars and garages for two years. They were things that, at 20, Ren had been as ill prepared to handle as Kerri was to experience them. "But these days, the donation of nine months in the womb doesn't necessarily make you a mother anymore."

Despite the difficulty of the last four years, Ren had never felt any bitterness about having to care for Kerri—just for the way Anita had damaged the young girl's psyche. It was hard not to release the anger rising in her throat as her mother attempted to claim the role Ren had played for so long.

"We could have a better life, Ren. I could be a mother, a *real* one. There's money... fifty thousand. Your daddy left it in your name for when you turned twenty five. We could get that money and be a family again." Anita's emotional words barely concealed her desperate tone. "I just wanted to bring us together... I could get Kerri and then I knew you would come."

It took Ren more than a moment to digest the words she'd heard. Discerning the root of the matter—there was money and *Anita* wanted it—was a much easier task than processing the fact that her father had thought of her and left the money without ever telling her. It was a one-two punch; the rage for the way her mother had shattered her peace here in Three Rivers and keening grief at the mention of her father's desire to take care of her long after his death.

Her stomach roiling, Ren held no illusions that her mother's desire to have the money that was rightfully hers was so they could be a family again. The cosmetic enhancements to Anita's face she'd noticed were only the beginning. It might be as easy to fall into the fairy tale with Anita as it was to fall into the one she'd submitted to with Dane, but the end result for this one would be disastrous. No amount of money could repair their broken family unit. There wasn't a single ray of hope to salvage it.

She wished she could feel sorry for the woman her mother had become, but Ren could only be grateful she'd made the right choice to take Kerri from her in the first place. She hoped she would be able to keep her, protect her from the clearly unstable monstrosity before her.

Had her father known how things would go after he died? Briefly, she wallowed in a long wave of grief, missing him more than she ever had. The Ren who had arrived in Three Rivers mere months ago, having struggled for the last four years would have taken the money and run. She could put a lot of distance between them with fifty thousand dollars, but now that she'd tasted happiness as a part of the Baylor family, she knew she would never be happy. Above all, her father's wish was for her to be happy, and even in death, he could provide that. With the money, maybe she could stand and fight for what *she* wanted out of life for once. It was a strange thought. *Thank you, Daddy. I love you.*

"So that's why you came all this way, now. To take what daddy left for me?" When she put it to words, it enraged her. She wanted to leap across the table and strangle the woman who offered her best impression of a sad smile to the daughter she had been taking from her entire life.

"I don't want to take it from you, I want *us* to have it."

Tempering her words carefully, Ren rose.

"*You* won't have it. And you won't have Kerri. I can promise you that. I'm done giving to you with no return. I have a life here and I'm done running. You can't take any of this away from me." She wanted to believe everything she was saying the same way she wanted so badly to believe Dane when he'd held her through the night and told her things would work out in their favor but she was quaking on the inside.

Anita's face abruptly changed from benevolent matriarch to screaming banshee, pounding her cuffed fists against the tabletop.

"You stupid spoiled bitch! Declan gave you everything, *everything*. There was nothing left for me! I *deserve* this for putting up with you, you ungrateful, needy little whore." Rage darkened Anita's features. "I saw that house. You're already going to have everything you want, you filthy slut! All you do is take from men and you leave nothing for other women!"

It took everything Ren had to maintain her composure as she backed away from the table, reluctant to turn her back on the viper that had once been her mother. Deputy Collins took a step forward, touching Ren's arm lightly.

"Mrs. Maddock, that's quite enough." His voice was authoritative and firm, but Anita kept screeching, incoherent now. At the door, Ren turned and took one final look at the woman. She had no idea how she was going to fulfill the promise she had made to her mother, but she knew she had to try.

TWENTY-SIX

BY THE TIME Ren got back to the ranch, the sun had set. She'd called ahead to let Dane know she would be too late to put the kids to bed. He hadn't been pleased, but recognizing that her biggest threat was sitting in the cell at the sheriff's department must have made things a little easier for him to swallow, because he didn't argue.

It was pushing ten o'clock and she'd burned half a tank of gas driving every road inside of the Three Rivers town limits. The driving brought her comfort; some of her best thinking happened when she had nothing better to do than guide the Jimmy around the curves of the road, the windows open with fresh air filtering through.

When she pulled into the yard of the Baylor ranch, she had developed a plan. She would stand and fight, but if she could not defeat her mother legally, she would take the money and run. She couldn't let Kerri fall back into her mother's care.

They would change their names, forge new identities, skip the country if they had to. It would hurt like hell to leave Dane here, and she knew the last thing her daddy would want her to do was run, but she couldn't see any other choice and she didn't want to bring any more pain to the Baylor family. They would try with the lawyer, with child protective services, and if they couldn't make those venues work, she would steal away in the night like she had so many times before. Protecting her heart would take a backseat to protecting her sister.

Most of the lights in the house were out as she crept in. There was a foil-wrapped plate with a note from Ella on the kitchen counter but Ren wasn't hungry. She moved through the house as quietly as she could, up the stairs to peer inside Kerri's bedroom door. She was in bed, asleep, with her nightstand lamp still turned on. Satisfied she was in one piece, she softly closed the door and moved through her bedroom to access the back stairwell. Both Gage and Dane's doors were partially opened and a dim light came from Dane's. She opted to poke her head inside of Gage's door to ensure his presence, and satisfied, turned for Dane's bedroom.

He was stretched out on the bed on his stomach, on top of the blankets. He still had his jeans and the bedside light on, like he hadn't planned on falling asleep, but the last couple of days had been long and exhausting for all of the residents of the Baylor home.

Ren took a couple of moments to drink him in, all sinewy, sun-kissed natural muscle and masculinity. She thought of what it would take away from her to have to leave him now. She'd broken her own rules and now she might have to pay the consequences.

She crossed the floor and crawled across the bed to press her lips to the base of his neck at the bottom of his hairline. It wasn't until she touched him that he stirred, rolled onto his side so he could face her and lifted his arm to usher her into his embrace.

"Hey. How'd it go?" He gave her a sleepy lopsided smile that made her heart clench and she reached down and cupped his jaw, drawing her mouth to his without any words.

Dane was slow to respond but game, dropping a hand to her hip and shuffling her closer across the bed without breaking the kiss. Ren sat up and shifted, straddling his waist. Urgently, and hands trembling, she pulled her shirt off over her head. She met his mouth for a brief, crushing kiss and then tipped back to get her fingers at the belt buckle which had left an impression on his bare abdomen.

"Hey." Dane covered her frantic hands with his. His still sleep-clouded eyes met hers and stilled the panic in her heart. Careful to move her with him, he shifted into a sitting position and took her hands in his, turning them over and kissing each palm gently, then dropping them to his shoulders. He framed her hips with his hands for just a moment, and then slid them over her skin to loosen the clasp of her bra.

Slowly, he drew the straps down her

shoulders and discarded the lacy undergarment. His eyes had not left hers the whole time and he brushed the back of his knuckles over her cheekbone, then slid his fingers underneath her hair, against her neck. Ren was acutely aware of the goosebumps rising on her skin and her blood rushing in her ears. Emotionally, she had settled but his soft touch had her body quaking with anticipation.

~

Dane brought her close, brushing his lips over hers, feather-light. His teeth grazed her lower lip and she opened to him, sweet and giving. What a marvel it was that this woman who had already had so much taken from her still had anything to give, especially to him. It was a blessing he didn't deserve.

There was an urgency in her tonight. She was scared, he could tell. He cursed himself for letting her go to the Sheriff's office alone today, but she had been insistent and she could be stubborn. Then she'd come in here, all wild eyed like an unhandled filly and he realized how scared he'd been, himself, for the last few days. Though the words hadn't crossed her lips, he was all too aware that her first instinct in the face of this kind of trouble was to run, and he couldn't live with that option.

He kissed her long and deep, giving more than he took. His words weren't enough to make her believe she was safe here; maybe he could express it in his touch. No matter what happened, she had a home here, with Kerri, or, God forbid, without. With him. With Gage. God knew these two particular Baylor men needed her as badly as anybody.

She shifted back again to work at the belt buckle and he let her this time, stroking her back lightly as he watched the rise and fall of her chest, the pulse throbbing at the base of her throat, the way a stubborn twist of auburn hair tumbled into her eyes as she focused. He was overwhelmed by the small details.

"You're so damn beautiful. Has anyone ever told you that?"

She looked up and the answer in her eyes near broke his heart. He took the curve of her jaw in his hand and drew her down for another kiss. She laughed with surprise as he rolled her onto her back and hovered above her before he made his way down her body, littering a trail of kisses over her porcelain skin. Didn't seem to matter how much sun she got here at the ranch, the only evidence of it were new freckles on her nose and shoulders.

"Let me show you." He deftly unbuttoned her jeans and slipped them off over her hips. The lacy panties slid down her thighs with the same achingly slow pace, and he was amused to find they matched the bra he'd discarded—he had been pretty sure that only happened on first dates and the pages of lingerie magazines. He didn't figure it mattered all that much since his favorite place to see them was on the floor.

Making the trek from her knee to the apex of her thighs with his mouth, he paused for just a breath before sliding his tongue along the luscious flesh of her core. She sat straight up, her eyes wide.

Dane looked up, meeting her eyes. "It's okay, sugar."

His hand on her stomach guided her to lie back on the bed again. He could feel her trembling breaths move through her body as he took another tentative taste of her. This time, she let loose a moan that told him she had no idea how sweet this could be. He couldn't wait to see the way her brow furrowed when she came, soaring high on ecstasy.

~

Ren could feel herself unraveling at her very seams. Sure she'd had lovers, but never like *this*. Dane took his time, worshiping her body in a way she'd never known, as if it was the greatest gift he'd ever gotten.

She pressed her head back against the pillow as his tongue took a third, then fourth swipe across the most sensitive part of her. She'd grown accustomed to slow building, monumentally cresting orgasms that left her completely useless at the end, and this one was rushing toward her like a stampede. Though she'd been a little embarrassed when he'd started, she pushed her hips up into him as she felt the pressure building under his tongue, striving to meet that runaway train of pleasure head on. Her fingers curled in his hair, against his scalp as she writhed under his attentions.

"Dane!" It was coming on too fast, and he reached up to gather one of her hands in his, never wavering from his mission. She sobbed aloud when she finally reached the point of collision, coming hard and fast and wholly unprepared.

He moved up her, the hard planes of his body sliding against the soft curves of hers. The friction sent a frisson of pleasure through her nerve endings which were already on high alert. Gliding her hands along the ridges of muscle on his abdomen, she circled around to his back and held him tight to her. The feel of his body against hers was something she'd never get tired of and she never wanted to have to let go. She could feel their hearts thudding in sync and thought for a moment this was exactly how things were meant to be.

Dane's devious mouth found her throat, his teeth nicking where his lips followed to soothe, and with her head dropped back, her body still trembling from her orgasm, he fit their bodies together in the most intimate way. A soft gasp let loose from her lips as he seated himself deep inside of her. Her fingers curled into the flesh of his shoulders and she let out a shaky breath.

"You okay?" He tipped his head back to catch her eye.

"Yes." Her voice was breathy, barely a whimper. She wanted it so badly she could taste it. "Please, Dane." She lifted her hips, shameless. If this was the last time they ever came together like this, she was going to make it count.

She could read a half a dozen emotions in his eyes but then he tucked his face against her neck and started moving, every single shift of his body sending a wash of pleasure through her. All too soon, she felt the familiar rise of ecstasy as he guided her toward her second orgasm.

He had clearly sensed her urgency. His movements were fast and tight, and soon he tensed.

"Shit." He rasped out, his lips against her throat.

She slid her hands down his sides to his ass, pressing him to her. Ren had no intention to back down now.

"Just let go, Dane."

TWENTY-SEVEN

DANE HELD HER afterward, his fingertips tracing light circles on her damp skin. She rested quietly with her head on his shoulder and one hand on his chest, her breathing soft and even but her eyes were wide open. Her mind was clearly elsewhere, and he knew he could blame her meeting with her mother today for that. He felt her swallow, and then again and when he looked down, she had tears in the corners of her eyes. Her hands were clenched into fists against his chest.

"Sugar, what's wrong?" He craned his neck to plant a kiss on the top of her head and ran a hand down her arm gently.

She sniffed, shook her head, dismissing the tears. How many times had she actually allowed herself to let go to grief and stress in the last four years? Their life on the road had been hard, and even in the months she had been here, he'd seen her put on a brave face plenty of times when anyone else would have shed at least a couple of tears.

He reached down and tipped her chin up so they could make eye contact.

"That was incredible, but it definitely wasn't worthy of tears. Spit it out."

She was silent a moment longer, collecting her thoughts.

"What if this doesn't work? I mean... what if they grant Anita custody? I can't live with that."

Frowning, Dane brushed a tear off of her cheek and her hair away from her face. Now that she'd opened up to talk, the tears flowed freely and she sniffed heavily, her nose filling up. Her vulnerability was a rare sight but he cherished every ounce of it just the same as all the other parts of her he'd seen over the last few months.

"You know that's not going to happen."

"I wish I could just trust that you can make everything happen the way I want it to, but I can't—not because I don't trust you but because I know life doesn't work that way. Not for me."

He paused, considered her words—she was right. He never imagined he'd be blindsided with Gavin's death and this whole other aspect to his life, but fate had a way of helping things work out in ways you couldn't imagine in the beginning.

"You've been taking excellent care of Kerri for four years, Ren. Nobody in their right mind is going to take her away from you and release her to your mother."

Ren made a strangled noise that just about broke his heart.

"But Banks was right. Four years ago, I did pretty much exactly what Anita did this week. What's the difference? With no documentation of her abuse, there isn't *anything* that makes me any better for Kerri than her."

"There is so." Dane squeezed her tight to his chest and pressed a reassuring kiss to her forehead. "There is *this*. This family, this home. A steady and dependable income, a nuclear structure. Anita can't offer that."

When she didn't reply, he tried again, his heart thudding like it would burst clean out of his chest.

"I love you, Ren. I know you might not be ready for that. Jesus, I might not be ready for that, but you belong with me. You and Kerri. I knew it the second you walked through my door." There. He'd put it out there for God and the world to hear and if she wasn't picking up what he was laying down, he would wait her out until she did. "And I'll do whatever it takes to make sure you stay here."

~

Ren was silenced by Dane's words. Flattered and heartbroken at the same time, she resisted the urge to sob right out loud and pressed her face against his chest. How was it that it was so much harder to be strong when there was someone else willing to bear the burden, even in part?

She had to pull herself together, she had no other option. He planned for her to stay but she had to make arrangements if she couldn't. Tomorrow, they would all be interviewed separately by social services, Sheriff Montgomery had explained, and that would set the precedence for the court hearing to determine official guardianship of Kerri. All of it made her anxiety spike through the roof. So many more hoops to jump through than to just hit the road. She would try, at the very least, so she could stay here with Dane. And failing that, she would go.

She let a long sigh out against the skin of Dane's chest as he stroked her hair lightly. She knew he wanted to hear those words back, but right now she just didn't have it in her. It would make things so much harder once she said them. Instead, she focused on the beating of his heart against her cheek, the temperature of his skin under her fingers, the rhythms and noises of his body just existing. It was something she wanted to commit to memory, just in case it was all she was left with. Sometime later, she drifted into a fitful sleep.

~

Morning came too early and Ren felt more hung over than she had the day after the dance hall. Unlike most other mornings, Dane hadn't gotten out of bed in the wee hours and here it was pushing eight and he was still holding her. Somehow, it had made the night pass easier. If she'd dreamt, she couldn't remember it and she was grateful, certain there could be nothing in the recesses of her subconscious except darkness.

Ren was surprised that he was still asleep but all of this had to have been as exhausting for him as it was for her, and he wasn't running on the same kind of scared adrenaline she was. She slid herself out of his arms as carefully as she could but he stirred when she pulled away. She gave him her best attempt at a reassuring smile and leaned across the bed to give him a kiss, pulling on her t-shirt and underwear before she crept up the stairs.

There was a gentle knocking on the main door as she slid into the room from the back stairwell. She frowned, crossing the floor quickly and pulled the door open to find Kerri standing there. The girl's hair and face were a mess and Ren could tell her sister likely had as fitful a night as she had.

"Come on in, sweetie." Ren held her arms open and Kerri went directly into them. Ren felt her face contort with the threat of a sob but she swallowed it down before her sister could see and ushered her further into the bedroom. "What's wrong?"

"Are they going to make me go with her?"

Ren frowned, settling her sister on the edge of her still made bed. If Kerri noticed it, she didn't say anything.

"No, they're not." Ren's voice was fierce as she clasped her sister's hand. "You're going to meet someone from social services today and they're going to ask you some questions about your life with me, and what your life was like with Anita. I want you to tell the truth, every time, just like Daddy taught us, okay?"

The girl nodded tearfully.

"You just tell them who you want your family to be, and why. Tell them what you remember from before we started living together. Tell them what life is like now, here with me. And Dane. He wants to help make sure you stay here, too."

This wasn't the first time Ren had faked this kind of confidence in front of Kerri, especially in the last few days, and she prayed the act still looked sincere. She ran her hand over her sister's hair and let out a long breath, giving Kerri a smile she hoped sent the right message.

"You want some breakfast?"

"I don't know if I could eat." Kerri's words were mumbled.

"I know, me either, but the boys will be hungry no matter what. Come on, let's go make some pancakes."

They went down the stairs and started to prepare breakfast for the four of them. It wasn't long before Gage and Dane joined them and it hardly took any time for the banter and playfulness between the four of them to resume the way it had been going all summer. Ren savored it. Like a real family.

TWENTY-EIGHT

REN TAPPED HER foot anxiously as she waited for Kerri to reappear. Dane sat beside her much as he had the day they found the children missing after their date, an arm over her shoulder. She crossed and uncrossed her arms, anxious just to see her sister's face at the end of the debacle.

Dane squeezed her shoulders lightly. "Would you relax?"

They were in the hall of the Sheriff's office again, and Ren had made up her mind that if she didn't have to see the inside of this building ever again in her lifetime, she'd be happy. Three Rivers was small enough, it seemed pretty much anything official transpired inside of these doors.

"They're keeping her an awful long time." Ren huffed.

"They're just crossing all their t's and dotting all their i's. Asking the right questions to make sure we won't have to do this over." The calmness in

Dane's voice was an anchor for her. She could have easily let her mind sift through all of the negative outcomes at a million miles an hour, but he centered her. She let out a long breath.

"You're right."

He chuckled softly, the sound further easing the anxiety in her bloodstream. "Of course I am."

Not two minutes later, Kerri emerged. Her furrowed brow indicated she had clearly had some anxiety during the interview but it eased as soon as she saw her sister. Ren rose and pulled Kerri into her arms tightly, swearing she wouldn't let her go. All too soon, though, they were being ushered into the interview room by the representative from social services, a middle aged man with a paunch and a pinstriped shirt. Ren's ran her hands over her sister's hair and pressed her forehead against Kerri's.

"We've got this, Ker-bear. Don't worry."

Ren was surprised when Dane moved with her, guiding her toward the room, never taking his arm off of her shoulders as Kerri took a seat with Deputy Collins in the waiting area. The social services officer who had introduced himself as Art Thompson made a motion to stop Dane from entering but the younger man's resolute expression stopped him.

"If it's all the same to you, Mr. Thompson, Ren doesn't have anyone else here to be with her."

Thompson pursed his lips but then allowed the pair entrance and took up his seat behind the desk as they sat in the chairs opposite. It reminded

Ren entirely too much of the night Sheriff Montgomery had reminded her that she had no legal right to Kerri, and she wondered if Art Thompson would be telling her the same thing today.

He shuffled through a few papers then looked up and cleared his throat.

"Well, Kerri unequivocally wants to stay with you, Ms. Maddock. She made that quite clear in her interview. She has absolutely no interest in residing with Mrs. Maddock."

Ren breathed a small breath of relief but she knew this was only half of the battle. Myrna Pierce had stopped by for coffee this morning before they'd come and had primed them that social services would also be interested in the type of home life Ren could provide.

Art Thompson continued.

"Obviously, we want to do what is in the best interest of the child in question, but I have a few other questions about the situation Kerri would be living in provided we grant you guardianship of your sister, Ms. Maddock."

"Yes, sir." Ren nodded, wetting her lips. She'd prepared the answers to the questions she imagined he would ask a million times.

"You can call me Art, Ms. Maddock. When you say 'sir', I look over my shoulder for my father." The man offered her a kind smile, clearly attempting to lighten the mood in the room.

"Okay."

"Ms. Maddock, do you hold permanent

employment?" Thompson read the question from a sheet in front of him.

Casting a brief glance at Dane, she nodded.

"Yes, I do. And a trust fund was set up through my father's life insurance that I am eligible to receive within the year, by my 25th birthday."

"And you have permanent arrangements for residence?"

"Yes, we have an agreement with the Baylors and live on the ranch."

"Is this permanent?"

Ren's stomach knotted. She knew all too well there was little in life that was permanent, least of all her living arrangements. Dane intercepted.

"Yes, Mr. Thompson, it is a permanent arrangement." Dane's big hand closed over her fidgeting fingers.

The social worker looked pointedly at their joined hands and shifted.

"It's my understanding the Maddocks haven't been in Three Rivers for long, Mr. Baylor..."

Ren glanced at Dane. She saw his jaw work and then he caught her eyes.

"I understand it appears that way, but Ren and I have been courting for quite some time. I promise you the home environment is stable. We're engaged to be married." Dane offered the man a reassuring smile and Ren nearly choked on her tongue. He didn't make eye contact but Dane squeezed her fingers again, prompting her to keep her mouth shut. "Kerri will start at Three Rivers High in September."

Thompson's eyes flicked to Ren as if to corroborate Dane's story but all she could do was nod dumbly and hope she looked convincing.

"I see." Thompson looked back at his paperwork and made a couple of notations. "Until the hearing, I will grant custody and temporary guardianship of Kerri to you, Ms. Maddock, and Mr. Baylor. Mrs. Maddock is obviously not in any position to be her guardian at this time, and you don't seem to pose a flight risk, Ms. Maddock, considering your *ties* to the community." At the word 'ties', the man peered over his glasses at Dane, and Ren was convinced he didn't buy Dane's story. She held her breath.

"The custody hearing will be in two weeks' time." The social worker rose from behind the desk and moved toward the door. "I suggest you bring your lawyer, Mr. Baylor, Ms. Maddock."

He held the door open as they stood and exited the office. Ren felt like her body and her brain were disconnected, as with a gentle touch at the small of her back, Dane guided her into the foyer of the Sheriff's office. He shook Thompson's hand and Ren did the same, barely thinking of the situation at hand but of the lie Dane had told. He couldn't have meant it, but if she needed to pretend to be engaged to Dane for the sake of keeping Kerri, that was exactly what she would do. It sounded better than running right now.

Suddenly, an enormous rush of relief overpowered Ren. It was only two weeks of peace, but compared to the life she had been living for the last four years, it sounded like a lifetime. Two weeks that wouldn't require her to look over her shoulder every thirty seconds or keep Kerri constantly in her line of sight.

As they passed by Sheriff Montgomery's door, Dane poked his head in. "Hey Banks. You'll call me if she makes bail, right?"

From where he had been going over paperwork, the young sheriff looked up at his childhood friend. "It isn't very likely... but of course. Have a good night, now."

Ren slipped her hand into Dane's as they left the office.

"The only person alive to pay her bail would be me." She said it as much to herself as to anybody else. A laugh bubbled up from deep inside of her chest and once she started, she couldn't stop. Dane opened the passenger side door of his truck and helped her in while she continued, finally throwing her head back and giving up to the laughter while he walked around the hood and got into the driver's seat. He took a look at her and shook his head with a smirk.

Five miles from the ranch, Ren finally reined herself in, her eyes and nose streaming. Sniffing a bit, she shook her head.

"That woman has never loved anyone. Not even my father. It's a wonder I even know how."

Reaching across the seat, Dane wordlessly closed her hand in his.

"I do, though," she said.

"I know you do." Dane's words were quiet.

"Someone who doesn't know how to love wouldn't have worked so hard to keep Kerri safe for the last four years, or sacrificed whatever semblance of a normal life she could have had to raise her. You can tell when you talk to her how much you love her. And Gage. I didn't know it was possible for that little boy to know more love than what our family gives him, but you waltzed in and showed him even more."

"And you." She watched him. She might not be able to say the three-little-words but he should know she reciprocated his feelings, even if she couldn't put it to words. He smiled and without taking his eyes off the road, lifted their hands to kiss the back of hers.

EPILOGUE

DANE WIPED HIS hands nervously on his jeans. *Jesus.* He hadn't had sweaty palms over a girl since middle school, and here he was, thirty two years old, and he couldn't get a handle on his nerves.

He'd saddled Maverick and Roxy and sent Finn to the house to get Ren. It had taken a little planning but he'd managed to set aside this block of time just for them. After what happened the last time they rode out, he wanted to change those memories for her.

Maverick swung his head to look at Dane, who was pacing a short four stride line back and forth across the floor of the barn. What was taking so long? For what felt like the fifteenth time, he checked his pocket to make sure he still had it. The horse thought it was a treat and without fail, every time Dane triple checked his pocket, Maverick nudged him for a treat.

After what felt like hours, Dane heard the door of the barn swing open and he released a long breath. It had been a crazy couple of weeks for the whole family. They were all just beginning to relax and settle into the security of knowing a judge had legally given permanent custody of Kerri to Ren and Anita would not be bothering them anytime soon.

"Hey, sugar," he greeted Ren as she came into view. A bemused expression covered her pretty face and it brought a smile out of him. His nerves ebbed away as she got closer and he took her in his arms and pressed a kiss to her lips. "Finn with the kids?"

They still took precautions because it made everyone feel better, even though Anita was still in custody, awaiting trial for the abduction of Gage. There were still a lot of 'what ifs' to contend with, but the stress and anxiety had begun easing out of Ren's face the second the judge had awarded them Kerri.

She nodded, casting her eyes to the saddled horses.

"What's going on?"

"You wanna go for a little ride with me?"

The slow smile that crept across her face as she stroked Roxy's neck warmed his heart. With everything going on, the last couple of weeks had seen few opportunities for them to spend time alone together, despite the fact they were now living as a family instead of a boss and employee.

"Finn's okay with staying with the kids?"

Dane nodded, gesturing to his saddlebags.

"I brought wine."

"What are we waiting for?"

The pleased expression on her face was unabashed and she slid the reins off of Roxy's neck to lead her out into the yard. Rex greeted them, wiggling with abandon as if he was in on the secret.

~

Ren swung her leg over Roxy's back and waited for Dane to do the same. He had paused, watching her over Maverick's saddle with an expression on his face she couldn't quite place. Every once in a while, she'd catch him staring at her. It wasn't unlike the period of time between the provisional custody they'd been given and the actual custody hearing, except during that time, she was convinced he'd been watching for signs that she would be packing her things and spiriting away in the night. It was different now, though. Less scared. Softer. More suspicious.

"You gonna stand there looking at me forever?" She cocked a brow at him and gestured to Maverick, who was now nosing Dane's pocket, looking for a treat.

Shaken from his reverie, Dane grinned. "Maybe."

She laughed as he mounted up. Dane reined Maverick toward the gate to the back pasture.

Exhaling deeply, Ren settled into Roxy's relaxed stride, riding knee to knee with Dane. She might not be as comfortable as the Baylors on horseback, but she was beginning to understand something Dane had told her in the early days about the outside of a horse being good for the inside of a man. She felt competent and safe with Roxy as a mount and she could almost feel the tension and stress of the last few weeks draining out of her arms and legs.

She recognized the trail they were taking almost immediately and tamped down the nerves that fluttered in her stomach when they crested the hill and saw the live oak they'd sat under the day Anita had taken Kerri and Gage. Dane reached over and slipped her hand into his.

"I thought we should make some good memories here."

The man had read her mind. She gave his hand a squeeze and let out a breath she hadn't realized would be shaky.

"Don't worry, Ren. Finn is with the kids."

They made it to the tree and dismounted, slipping the bridles off of the horses, who happily moseyed off to graze while they set up under the oak. Dane assembled a blanket, two glasses and a bottle of wine he'd produced from his saddle bags, then sat with his back against the tree, inviting her to slide into the v his legs made. She settled with her back against his chest.

While leaving the kids alone did make her nervous, she was happy for this quiet time together. They'd had enough drama in the last month to fill a lifetime, and she was beyond prepared for the routine that school starting would bring.

Dane carefully moved her hair to the side and

pressed his lips to the sweet spot behind her ear. Her fingers, resting on his jean-clad thighs, tightened just a bit. She could feel the hot exhalation of breath and his features change as he smiled against her skin. He shifted, and then she saw him slide a flash of white gold and diamond onto one of those fingers. By the time he'd slid it home on her left ring finger, her hands were trembling so hard he covered them with his own.

"I know you thought I was telling fibs to the social worker to sway him in our favor."

Her heart was racing and a huge lump formed in her throat as she turned her hand over in his, examining the ring. It had a large diamond flanked by smaller ones in a curved channel setting of white gold. The ring was elegant, beautiful, and probably the most expensive piece of jewelry she'd ever seen, let alone worn. She wanted to take it off and tell him he didn't mean it. They'd told a white lie to the social worker to increase the likelihood of him letting Kerri live with them. That's all it had been— a lie. But the ring on her finger *wasn't* a lie.

When she didn't reply, Dane continued.

"We can have a long engagement, if you want. But I want you to know I'm serious about the little family we have here, and the life we can have together. I love you, and I can't imagine my life without you and Kerri in it." He squeezed her hand lightly. "So I'm asking you, Ren Maddock... Maybe not today or tomorrow, but someday in the not-so-distant future, if you would be my wife."

Ren's eyes filled as he spoke and when he

finished with that word—*wife*, they spilled over. It wasn't the ring, or the question, it was the idea that he had picked *her*. Of all the women in the world, he had chosen her, first. She hadn't been picked first for a single thing since her father had passed away. She turned in his arms, pressing a gentle kiss to his lips. Her whole body melted into it as his hands slid up her back and he held her to him. All too soon, he broke the kiss.

"So you never gave me an answer." His tone was teasing as he tipped his head back with a smile to catch her eyes.

"Yes. Yes, of course yes."

ABOUT THE AUTHOR

Amity Lassiter lives in Eastern Canada with her herding dog, her barn cat, two horses and her Mister. She has loved telling stories her entire life and even before she could write could be found in her grandmother's basement, reciting fiction into an ancient cassette recorder.

The most influential author in Amity's life would be Peter S. Beagle, the author of The Last Unicorn, who introduced her to her first achingly impossible love story and made her believe in magic. She met, and shared the most surreal small talk with Beagle in May 2014.

She loves critters, coffee, and cowboys—and she still believes in unicorns.

You can find more from Amity Lassiter online at www.amitylassiter.com